THE HOUSE BY THE SHORE

SEA BREEZE COVE BOOK ONE

FIONA BAKER

Published in the United States of America

First Edition, 2021

fionabakerauthor.com

CHAPTER ONE

"Where on earth did my keys go? How did they move themselves? Did they grow legs in the middle of the night and just walk away?" Charlotte Winters muttered as she frantically shuffled through the junk mail and random items cluttering up the stand in her entryway. "I can't *afford* to be late. Not today!"

She wasn't sure how time had gotten away from her so badly. One moment she was relaxed, making her coffee and listening to a great audiobook, and the next she was behind schedule, scrambling to make it out the door. Today was going to be a big day—Charlotte's calendar was full, and her boss had mentioned some important news was coming. Maybe her nerves had gotten to her without her realizing it.

"They're here, babe!"

Her boyfriend came into the entryway with her keys on his finger. Peter was still in his pajama pants and a t-shirt, his hair messy from sleep since he had gotten up a half hour after her. Charlotte almost envied him for a moment, before remembering with a guilty pang that he would rather be going to work too. Despite the fact that Chicago had a number of universities and museums, Peter was having a hard time finding work as a linguistics professor.

Charlotte knew this was one reason her mom and sister didn't fully approve of him. But she and Peter had been together a while now. *She* knew that he was smart and a hard worker; it was just a matter of time before something clicked for him.

"You're the best, thanks!" Charlotte took her keys and tucked them into her purse, double checking that she also had her phone and wallet. Wallet, yes; phone, no. It was still in the kitchen where she'd left it next to her coffee. She couldn't forget her coffee. "What time is your interview, again?"

"Eleven thirty at the Historical Society. I'm still nervous. I'm prepared, but maybe they'll throw me a curveball."

"You'll do great. You know more than basically

anyone about the history of all the linguistic changes in the Midwest." Sipping her coffee, Charlotte came back into the entryway. It had finally cooled down during her rush to find her keys.

"I hope I do." Peter ran a hand through his hair, looking a bit nervous. Charlotte knew he was worried about getting his hopes up just to be disappointed again, and she wished she could promise him he'd get the job. She wanted so much for him to achieve the success he deserved and craved.

"I know you do. That was what drew me to you on one of our first dates, remember? The one at the coffee house connected to that cute bookstore? You told me all this cool stuff about how immigrants from Germany had shaped the dialects in the region until I forgot what time it was."

Charlotte had known she was going to fall in love with him on that date at the coffee shop. Their mutual love of language and books had taken them into two different careers—her into publishing, and him into a PhD in linguistics—so they'd had plenty to talk about. They had discussed their favorite books and languages for so long that the baristas had needed to kick them out. After that, they'd gone to a bar and kept talking until past midnight. It was one of Charlotte's fondest memories.

"Yeah, I remember." Peter's smile didn't quite reach his eyes.

"So you'll kill it." Charlotte slipped on her favorite flats, which she could finally break out now that there wasn't snow or slush on the ground. She wished she could stay and give him the support he needed, but she was running late.

"Thanks, Charlotte." Peter smiled again, more brightly this time, and gave her a quick peck on the lips. "Have a good day. And good luck to you too."

Reassured, Charlotte rushed outside and toward the train, thankful that the spotty weather of spring was finally settling into the pleasant, consistent warmth of summer. It wasn't too hot yet, but in a few weeks, it was going to be.

She slipped onto the El just before the door closed, her breathing labored. No one on the train looked twice at her—she figured that they had all been running late at least once before too. She listened to more of her audiobook while casually flipping through her full work email inbox. There was already so much to take care of—upcoming book launches, presentations to the sales team, a seemingly infinite pile of little tasks too.

A short time later, she walked into the office. Her cubicle mate was already there.

"Good morning, Charlotte." He shot her a smile.

"Morning, Aaron!" Charlotte flopped into her chair, booting up her computer. "Busy day ahead, right?"

"Yeah, as always. It seems like today's extra stuffed with meetings. Orson seems extra stressed."

Aaron glanced behind them, where Charlotte could see the heads of the editorial director and publisher over the edge of their cubicles. It wasn't that unusual, but the way Orson and Candice had their heads bowed together, slight furrows in their brows, made her pause. Both of them were usually upbeat, even first thing in the morning.

Charlotte's stomach twisted a little bit. *What's going on?* she wondered. Her boss had alluded to big news today; was it going to be bad? Or was it just something that was going to shake things up in the company for the better?

She shook off her suspicions and dove head-first into her work, answering emails from authors, coordinating with the production team, and going to meetings. By the time lunch rolled around, she was starving and tired. In her rush to get out the door, she hadn't even grabbed a granola bar to eat on her commute.

"Hey, Charlotte? Can you come in here for a bit?"

Charlotte was just about to head out to grab something from a food truck, but one look at Candice's face made her gut tighten.

"Yeah, of course."

As Candice shut the door behind her, Charlotte's suspicion that this news wasn't good crystalized in her mind. Usually the publisher was all smiles, even when books she loved tanked, but today there was tension in her eyes.

"So, the company hasn't had a great quarter," Candice began as she sat down. "Which I think you're aware of."

"Yes, vaguely." Charlotte had seen the sales for their latest season of books and they were way down despite hopes that there would be a breakout hit. The advances they'd given were way too high in contrast with the low sales.

"Unfortunately we're going to have to lay a few people off as a result," Candice continued, not meeting Charlotte's eye. "You've been an amazing asset, but we have to downsize your department. We have to let you go."

Charlotte blinked, the breath leaving her body for a moment. When she'd set out this morning knowing that today was a big day, it hadn't occurred to her for a moment that this was what was going to happen. She'd thought "big" meant a new high profile author or a new hire, not this.

"Oh," was all she could think to say.

"I'm so sorry, Charlotte. I wish I could keep everyone, but it's just not feasible at the moment." Candice folded her hands on her desk.

"It's okay. I understand." Charlotte struggled desperately to maintain her composure, despite how hurt she felt. She was good at her job and the authors she worked with loved her. But there was nothing she could do to change the financial reality her company was going through.

"I'll connect you with HR who can tell you more details." Candice stood and shook Charlotte's hand, giving her a sympathetic smile. "If you need a recommendation, I'd be happy to give you one. Feel free to take the rest of the day off if you need to."

"Thanks, Candice." Charlotte stood too, swallowing. "I think I'll take you up on that offer."

Still stunned, Charlotte gathered her purse and a few of the little personal items she'd kept at her desk. *Might as well start packing*, she thought to herself as she tucked the items into her bag. Most of her coworkers had left for lunch so at least she didn't have to face them yet.

She took the elevator downstairs and headed toward the El again. Her favorite food cart was on the way and she figured that if there was any right time to indulge in a kebab platter with fries, it was now. Just smelling the area around the cart made her mouth water—the spices and meat mingled together in a way that could have woken her up from even the deepest sleep. Feeling slightly less shattered thanks to the promise of a feel-good lunch, she continued her walk to the train.

She was going to miss this area—there were a lot of great shops and places to get coffee. With the warm weather, a lot of restaurants had reinstated their outdoor seating and people were out enjoying it. As she people-watched, a familiar face caught her eye at a restaurant patio across the street. Peter? It was definitely him. He was wearing the blue plaid button-down that she had gotten him for Christmas last year. Charlotte felt a rush of relief. Sharing her news with her partner and best friend would help take away some of the sting. Perhaps they could wallow in their unemployment status together.

As she approached the crosswalk, Charlotte

paused in confusion. *Who's that woman he's with? Is he still in his interview?* Glancing at her phone, she saw it was close to one, so if it was his interview, it was running long. *Maybe he got the job, and his new boss has taken him to lunch!*

But then, Charlotte watched in horror as Peter reached up and swiped something off the woman's lip, making her laugh. As he leaned across the table and kissed the unfamiliar woman, Charlotte's heart dropped to her feet.

She stopped dead in the middle of the crosswalk. She couldn't believe what she was seeing. A passerby's annoyed grumble shook her out of her stupor and she kept walking until she was standing on the other side, close to the scene which was rapidly unravelling what remained of the world she had woken to that morning.

There had to be a logical explanation for what she was seeing, besides the one that seemed the most obvious. The one thing she didn't want it to be. Maybe it was his interview after all, somehow. Or maybe it was something else, like an act of some sort.

But when she caught Peter's eye, his shoulders tensed and guilt flashed across his face. Charlotte swallowed the lump in her throat. Her instincts were spot on, as much as she wished they weren't.

She gathered herself as she came closer to the table.

"Hi, Peter," she said coolly. "I didn't think I'd find you here."

The woman he was with looked up at Charlotte, understanding dawning on her face. Her cheeks went red and she looked at Peter.

"I...have to go to the restroom?" She nearly pushed her chair over backward as she got up quickly, hustling inside and leaving Charlotte and Peter alone.

Peter ran a hand over his face and Charlotte took the vacant seat. Neither spoke, until the long pause became so uncomfortable that Charlotte had to break it.

"So this was your interview?" she asked, her quiet, controlled voice signaling the devastation which simmered beneath her words. With so many people around, she didn't want to make a huge scene, even though on the inside she was breaking down into tears.

"No, it wasn't." Peter sat back in his seat, sighing. "It went well, though."

Still holding her emotions in a vise-like grip of control, Charlotte bit back a snarky response. She had no idea how to respond to that blip of pleasant news in a situation which she was quickly realizing was as dire as her gut was screaming at her. In other circumstances, she would've been thrilled for him, but she couldn't muster up any positive feelings toward him at the moment.

"So who is she?" Charlotte folded her trembling hands in her lap. "Not a friend, I'm guessing?"

"No. We're more than that." Peter took a long drink of water.

Charlotte watched him, waiting for him to continue. To beg her to forgive him. To tell her that this was the biggest mistake he'd ever made. But he just looked off into the distance, an inscrutable look in his eyes.

"I've fallen in love with her, Charlotte," he said, looking down at the table. "I think we should break up."

Charlotte's mouth dropped open and she let out a laugh of disbelief. Was she really hearing him correctly? Her control began to slip. "*Now* you think we should break up? Now that you've already fallen in love with someone else? And only after I caught you kissing her in public? This morning, everything was completely fine!"

Peter took his glasses off and rubbed the bridge of his nose, a tell-tale sign that he was getting a headache or overly stressed. He lowered his voice, a not-so subtle pointer that she had raised hers and it was embarrassing. Charlotte couldn't care less.

"I've been wanting to tell you for the past few weeks, but I wasn't sure how to broach the topic. It was pretty gradual, too. We met at the coffee shop where I go to work on job applications." Peter slid his glasses back on. "One minute, things were platonic but then suddenly, they weren't."

"'Suddenly they weren't'? What is that supposed to mean?" Charlotte sniffed. "Have we not been spending enough time together?"

"Maybe that's part of it. You've been so busy with work too and stressed out that I didn't want to add to that."

Charlotte ran her hands over her face. "That was supposed to be a rhetorical question. We spend a lot of time together when I'm not at work. Sure, my schedule's been busy but it's not like I'm working until midnight every single night."

Not that my work schedule matters anymore, she thought. She remembered her instinctive need to share with Peter the news that she'd been laid off, but now it felt like adding insult to injury. He had already fallen in love with someone else and there was a good chance that he'd get the job he had interviewed for. In the space of minutes, their roles had been reversed and they had nothing left in common.

The silence that came over the table was deafening.

"I didn't want to hurt you, Charlotte." Peter adjusted his glasses again, the lenses making the sincerity in his eyes feel even more potent. Somehow, that made Charlotte's heart hurt even more.

Charlotte finally let the tears fall from her eyes. "Well, you did, Peter."

She pushed back from the table so abruptly that her chair bumped into the empty one behind it. A cab was heading down the road, so she hailed it and climbed inside without looking back. Thankfully, the driver didn't ask her what was wrong as she quietly cried in the back seat.

Stepping inside their shared apartment felt like a slap in the face, especially knowing that he had been seeing this woman for at least a few weeks and probably longer. *Has he seen her here, while I've been at work?* On the wall was the picture they had taken together after he got his PhD, and a framed selfie they'd taken on a hike was squeezed next to the clutter that she had rifled through that morning. She put the photo face-down and went to the bedroom to pack up a bag, hardly caring what she threw in her duffel.

When she was done, she called her younger sister. "Hey, Nina. I need to crash at your place for a while. Is that okay?"

Nina didn't ask any questions, for which Charlotte silently blessed her. "Sure hon. You've got the key, so head over anytime. I'll bring home some extra wine. It sounds like you need it."

Charlotte had to smile a little bit, even though the heavy knot in her stomach was still weighing her down. Nina knew her well.

A short while later, she let herself inside Nina's apartment with her spare key and dumped her bag in the corner of the living room. Her feel-good lunch was cold by now, but still delicious and flavorful. With her belly full, she fell asleep on the sofa for a while, waking with a start as Nina bustled into the living room, home from her current job of freelancing at a marketing firm.

"I bought a whole box of chardonnay," Nina chirped, holding up the bag. "And some snacks."

"You're the best, Nina."

"Don't thank me. I could hear just how sad you sounded and I fully intend for us to drown your sorrows and smother them in calories. You'll regret it tomorrow, but you'll feel better tonight. Hold on, let me go change." Nina put the box of wine down on the counter and headed back to her room.

Charlotte shuffled over to the kitchen, feeling as if this day had lasted three times as long as any other. It was still Tuesday, but in Charlotte's head, it was already Friday. Nina had bought bags of white cheddar popcorn, chips, and chocolate covered pretzels, which Charlotte mixed together in a big bowl. She put it on the table along with the wine and two stemless glasses.

"Okay, tell me everything," Nina said, flopping down on the couch so hard that her messy dark bun flopped back and forth. Charlotte took a deep breath and decided it was better to just dive straight in without sugar-coating anything. There really was nothing to sugar coat.

"First, I got laid off. The company had a bad quarter and they had to downsize our department." Charlotte grabbed a handful of the DIY trail mix and stuffed it into her mouth so she could feel *something* besides numbness. It was good, but not a great distraction. It made it difficult to talk, but strangely that made it easier to share what she had to say. "And then when I was walking back to the train, I caught

Peter with another woman at a restaurant, sitting outside for everyone to see."

"No!" Nina gasped. "Seriously?"

"Seriously." Charlotte laughed humorlessly. "And I expected him to beg for forgiveness, but instead he just said that he'd fallen in love with this other woman and was breaking up with me."

Nina's hand tightened on the throw pillow in her lap. "I can't believe him."

"Me either." Charlotte chased the last bits of food in her mouth with wine. She had already decided to take the next day off too since she had so much paid leave saved up, so she could drink as much wine as she wanted. "Apparently they met at a coffee shop where he was working on his job applications. He said it was platonic until it suddenly wasn't."

"What is that even supposed to mean?" Nina narrowed her blue-green eyes. "Platonic until it wasn't? Isn't that true of anything? Like you're doing something until you aren't? Baking cookies, riding a bike, whatever?"

"That's exactly what I was thinking!" Charlotte said, sitting up. "And he had the nerve to say that he was going to tell me weeks ago, but he was afraid of hurting me."

"Seriously?" Nina scoffed. "And he thought that sitting outside with another woman in the vicinity of your job, where he could stumble upon your coworkers, wasn't going to hurt? What a royal jerk!"

"I know." Charlotte felt a few tears spill over. "I don't even know what to do."

"You don't have to think about it right now, okay?" Nina reached over and squeezed Charlotte's arm. "Let's just take an evening so you can decompress. Some trashy TV will help."

Charlotte wiped her eyes and nodded. Nina grabbed her remote and turned on the TV. Anything with a hint of a happy relationship was out, so they settled on a truly terrible reality TV show about a family with fifteen kids and their farm in the middle of Wyoming.

It was a good distraction, finally, and Charlotte found herself swept up in the staged drama of it all. Charlotte's phone buzzed on the table and she jumped, hoping it wasn't Peter. It wasn't; it was her mother. With a pang, she realized that part of her had thought it *might* be her now ex-boyfriend, calling to beg forgiveness.

"Hey, Mom," Charlotte said, hoping she sounded more put-together than she felt.

"H-hey, Char," her usually composed mother

said. The distress in her tone was obvious, and Charlotte immediately shelved her own troubles, relieved that something else could take priority, front and center in her mind.

"Is everything okay? I'm here with Nina and I'm putting you on speaker." Charlotte held the phone between the two of them as her sister leaned in, concern shining in her eyes. "What's going on?"

"I just got some bad news. Your Aunt Jean has passed away."

CHAPTER TWO

Charlotte found the downtown office where Aunt Jean's will was going to be read incongruously cheerful. There were fresh flowers, plenty of light streaming in through floor to ceiling windows, and sleek, modern desk spaces.

In any other circumstance or at any other time, Charlotte would have appreciated the ambiance, but in the few days since the wheels flew off her life, she hadn't been able to feel anything but unsettled. Even staying with Nina, who had been amazingly supportive since everything happened, hadn't steadied her as much as she anticipated.

Many of the things that felt like "her" were suddenly gone—her job, where she had worked for years, her relationship, her apartment. Being single and without the job that she loved made her realize just how much she had been going through the motions in life. Now she wasn't sure what to do with herself.

"Hi, come on in," Jean's estate lawyer, Greg said, holding the door open to his office for Charlotte, Nina, and their mother Melissa. "Have a seat."

Charlotte sat between her mother and sister, who were equally as somber. All of them wanted to get this meeting over with—as much as Charlotte loved her aunt, this reminder that she had passed was the last thing she wanted. Greg shuffled through papers on his desk for a little bit before sliding on his reading glasses.

"So, Melissa, Nina, and Charlotte." Greg looked at each of them over the rim of his glasses. "Jean has left you each thirty thousand dollars. The same sum has gone to a pet rescue organization in Sea Breeze Cove, Massachusetts."

Charlotte nodded. Aunt Jean had always loved animals, so she wasn't surprised at the donation.

"Jean has also left all of you her waterfront cottage in Sea Breeze Cove," Greg continued. "Her belongings within the house can be split between the three of you as you see fit."

Charlotte's eyebrows rose. Her aunt had loved

her little cottage, which they all used to visit every summer when she was growing up. There was no way Jean would let it go to someone outside the family, but it was still a bit of a shock for Charlotte to find herself inheriting part of the property.

Greg continued talking about the rest of Jean's assets, but Charlotte only paid a little attention.

"Do you have any questions?" Greg asked, tapping the edges of his papers against his desk.

Charlotte glanced at her mother, who seemed to be absorbing the information, then at Nina, who looked back at Charlotte.

"Not at the moment, no," Charlotte said for all of them.

"Okay, then." Greg stood and shook each woman's hand. "If you have any further questions, feel free to give me a call or send an email."

"Thank you," Melissa said as they walked out.

They were all quiet on the way to the elevator, the only sound being the click of Melissa's wedge heels on the floor. Charlotte glanced at Nina as Melissa politely greeted someone on the elevator, as if nothing was wrong. Being her daughters, both of them could tell that she was anything but fine.

But that was Melissa. She wasn't the type of woman to openly weep or have a single hair out of place. Even today, she was wearing a tasteful blue sheath dress, her dark hair in a chignon and her makeup applied just enough to highlight her features without calling attention to herself.

Charlotte, in comparison, had only been able to pull on some dark pants and a slightly rumpled blouse. She had only managed to put some moisturizer on her face and twist her damp hair into a bun. The only sign that Melissa was out of sorts was the slight tension in her brow that didn't go away, even with a cordial smile.

"Why don't we get something to eat?" Nina asked, shooting Charlotte another glance.

"That sounds like a great idea," Charlotte added.

Melissa wasn't going to open up to them, at least verbally, But both of them wanted to support her, even if she made it difficult to get past her walls.

"Okay." Melissa nodded. "Let's go somewhere around here."

* * *

They settled on a restaurant a few blocks away, a farm-to-table restaurant that Charlotte had heard good things about from friends. They settled in at their table, ordering the special of the day—ginger-glazed salmon with roasted Brussels sprouts, prosciutto and baby potatoes. After eating nothing but snacks and pizza for the past few days, Charlotte needed something that didn't come out of a bag or from a delivery guy.

No one spoke until the waiter took their menus away and brought back some iced tea.

"I think we should sell the cottage," Melissa said after taking a sip of her tea. "Since we're all here in Chicago, it doesn't make much sense to keep it."

"Yeah, that makes sense. Trying to coordinate renters or something like that from here seems like more trouble than it's worth." Nina swirled her straw in her drink. "But we'll have to figure out the best way to sell it."

"True..." Melissa blinked, trying to think the problem through. "I don't think it'll be that difficult of a task. The location is great and there's the guest house that could also bring in income for someone."

Charlotte's mind whirled as they discussed the merits of selling it now as it was, or fixing it up. The cottage had a special place in Charlotte's heart. She had spent so many summers there, enjoying the beach and the beautiful scenery. It had even been beautiful in the winter when they visited then, the cold air fogging her breath as they had walked on the empty beaches. They had stopped going when Charlotte was fourteen, but that didn't make the place any less special to her.

She didn't want to let the cottage go. She had already lost Jean—both time with her in the past and now, forever—and she knew she wouldn't forgive herself if she lost the cottage too.

"I'll buy your parts of the house from you," Charlotte blurted. "I want to keep it in the family. I can go live there."

Both Melissa and Nina stopped, staring at Charlotte with wide eyes. Nina's shock faded first.

"I think that could be a great idea. A nice adventure for you," Nina said, taking a freshly baked roll from the basket a waiter had discreetly slipped onto the table. "I'll sell you my share for twenty bucks."

"I think so too." Charlotte tore a piece of bread in half. Nina knew just how unsettled she had been feeling, so her abrupt declaration probably hadn't blindsided her. "And twenty bucks? You sure?"

"I'm sure. You deserve to take a new step."

Melissa took a roll as well, cutting into it instead of ripping it in half like Nina did. Charlotte waited for her response, taking her mother in. The sadness on her shoulders was still there, but so was a new layer of skepticism.

Charlotte knew the look well—Melissa always had strong opinions on Charlotte's life choices. When Charlotte had chosen to be an English major, Melissa had tried to guide her toward law school instead of publishing, since it was more lucrative. Once Charlotte had got into publishing, Melissa's feedback had shifted to her relationships and other small things. Her opinions were always formed and given out of love and never expressed in a mean way, but that didn't stop them from making Charlotte bristle a little bit.

"It's a little abrupt, don't you think? Crazy, almost?" Melissa asked. "Moving to the beach on a whim doesn't seem like the most level-headed idea when you have a career and a relationship."

"I don't have either anymore," Charlotte said slowly.

"What?" Melissa's eyes widened again. "What happened?"

"I got laid off and broke up with Peter." Charlotte didn't want to get into the details of the breakup with her mother at the moment. That would have derailed the conversation entirely into Melissa's feelings about Peter. "So there isn't much keeping me here."

"Oh." Melissa blinked, her eyebrows rising. She had never been particularly fond of Peter, but surprisingly, she refrained from launching into an *I told you so* speech. Instead, she just pursed her lips and said, "Well, I suppose it's not such a crazy idea after all then. I'll sell you my part too at the same price as Nina's share."

"Really?" Charlotte finally felt a glimmer of something that wasn't sadness or hurt for the first time since she'd discovered Peter's infidelity.

Her mother nodded. "Yes, really."

Charlotte could hardly believe it. On Monday, she had been debating whether to buy a new couch for the apartment she shared with Peter and fussing over emails on her commute, and now she would be picking up and moving to an entirely different state.

This was really happening. She was moving to Massachusetts.

CHAPTER THREE

"Alright, that's the last thing," Briggs said, loading the last of his few possessions into his pickup truck.

It was hardly at full capacity. All he needed were his clothes, a few necessities that were too expensive to regularly replace like kitchenware and some trusty appliances, and his toolkit. The rest he either went without entirely or picked up wherever he landed next.

"Wow, already?" His friend asked. "When you asked for a little help packing up, I set aside a whole afternoon."

"Yep. At least you have the rest of the day to relax if you want to." Briggs pushed his things into the truck a little bit more to be safe. "Help me with the tarp, would you?"

Colin grabbed the dark green tarp from its spot on the grass and tossed it over the truck bed. It was well-worn, but still sturdy from other trips Briggs had taken from town to town.

"It's a good thing you travel light. This tarp's a perfect fit," Colin said, looking around for some rope. "Where are you heading next?"

"Down the coast, I think," Briggs said, finding the ropes and handing one to Colin. "The winter up here in Maine has me craving something much warmer. "

Colin laughed, tying down one side of the tarp. "Yeah, Bangor in the winter isn't most people's cup of tea. But summer's not too bad besides some mosquitos and a few really hot days."

"Yeah, I know." Briggs secured the tarp on his side and gave it an extra tug to make sure it would hold as he drove. "But the further south I go, the more of the year I'll have to enjoy not freezing my butt off. It feels like winter lasts forever up here."

"True, true." Colin finished up on his side too, laughing a little. "But all you need is a nice fireplace and lots of layers to get you through those last stretches of cold days."

"That's what you say, but in reality the cold can just seep into your bones before you know it." Briggs smiled. "And then it's hard to shake. I'd heard that Maine winters were rough, but I thought I could handle it pretty easily with what I had. I was dead wrong, so I'll take more time without winter, thanks."

Colin tucked his hands into his pockets and came around to Briggs's side of the truck. "I get the feeling that you never stay in one place long, so I'm not too surprised that you're leaving. I bet you'd head out even if Bangor had the most beautiful weather you'd ever seen for sixty percent of the year."

Briggs shrugged, leaning up against the side of his truck. It was true—he had only stayed in Bangor for about six months, but he was already itching to move on despite all the area had to offer. He just wanted a change of pace and didn't want to get into it further. He liked Colin, but Briggs wanted to keep a lot of things close to his chest.

Colin sighed, and said, "I'm not sure what's eating at you and I don't want to pry, but I hope you get whatever you need wherever you're going. And keep in touch."

"Will do. Thanks, man," Briggs said, shaking Colin's hand. "Take care."

"You too."

Briggs hopped into his truck and headed out. A new town, a fresh start. He really didn't know where he was going to end up—he just wanted to head somewhere to the south. Somewhere smaller and quieter maybe, with a little more sun. He was going to miss Colin and some of the other friends he'd made in his short time in Bangor, but it was time to move on. It was better to leave now before he got too attached to the place or any of the people.

The weather was too nice to sit inside the stuffy car with the windows rolled up, so he opened them and sighed, letting the fresh air wash over him. He knew that bouncing from place to place wasn't going to stop his pain from following him, but for now, it was his only option.

"Can you see out of the back of here?" Nina asked Charlotte as she examined the stuffed trunk of her sister's car.

"Yup!" Charlotte shut the trunk and stepped back up onto the curb. "It's like Tetris—I've left just enough to see."

"Good." Nina pulled Charlotte into a hug, squeezing her tightly. She was so proud of Charlotte for shaking everything up. Charlotte was never the type to do anything drastic. "You'll text me at rest stops, right?"

"Of course I will." Charlotte gave Nina's back one more rub before pulling back.

"I'll miss you so much." Nina felt herself getting a tiny bit choked up. The past week since Charlotte had lived with Nina had been filled with sadness, definitely, but it had made Nina realize just how much she loved her sister.

"I'll miss you too. But you don't have to be a stranger." Charlotte gently tugged Nina's dark ponytail, just like she did when they were kids. "Come visit sometime."

"I will." Nina smiled, though she felt a tinge of envy at Charlotte's bravery too. "Is Mom not coming to say goodbye?"

"No, we said our goodbyes yesterday." Charlotte crossed her arms over her chest and sighed. "She definitely doesn't like this idea."

"Whatever." Nina waved her off. "We can't let Mom dictate our lives. If we did, we'd be like rigid little robots with our calendars planned out to the letter for the next five years."

Charlotte relaxed a little. "Yeah, true."

"She wants us to make the perfect choice every

time, but who can even do that? Sometimes things get messy whether you plan for it or not," Nina said.

"Case in point—my life right now." Charlotte smiled a little. "You can't plot out everything because you can't plan for everything. How was I supposed to know that Peter would cheat on me and that I'd get laid off on the same day? And what would I have done if Jean hadn't left us the cottage?"

"Exactly." Nina checked the time. "You should probably hit the road before traffic gets bad around here."

"I should." Charlotte opened her arms again and Nina stepped in for one last hug. "Thanks for all your help, Nina."

"No problem. That's what sisters are for, right?"

Charlotte gave her one last little smile before sliding into her car and driving off to the new chapter in her life.

CHAPTER FOUR

Charlotte rolled down her car's windows, taking in the clean air as she got closer to Sea Breeze Cove. The drive from Chicago to Massachusetts had gone smoothly despite the back of her car being packed to the gills with everything she owned. She hadn't wanted to divvy up her furniture with Peter, and besides, Jean's cottage was already furnished. If she wanted to buy new furniture in the future, she could.

She smiled as she saw another sign for Sea Breeze Cove in the distance. Finally. After a few days of driving, she was excited to settle in. The scenery became more and more beautiful, with glimpses of the ocean and sand dunes interspersed between old trees along the highway.

It still felt the same as it had when she used to

come to the town every summer until she was fourteen. They abruptly stopped going around then. She hardly saw Jean after that for reasons she wasn't quite sure of—there seemed to be a rift between Jean and her mother. Their phone calls abruptly stopped, and Melissa never updated them on how Jean was doing. Eventually Charlotte and Nina stopped asking as frequently. Either way, Charlotte felt bad about it, especially now that Jean was gone.

In what felt like no time at all, she was in Sea Breeze Cove. Seeing it again after all this time brought a rush of memories back to her. There were the places she loved and remembered, like a little shop with all sorts of handmade soaps, and a little seafood shack that had the best lobster rolls she'd ever had. Her mother had loved getting coffee at a little café on the side of town closest to Jean's house before they walked along the beach. Charlotte smiled to see the café was still there.

Charlotte sighed, drumming her fingers on the steering wheel when she came up to a stop sign. She and Nina used to be so much closer to their mother then. They would have girls' nights where they built a big fire on the beach and roasted marshmallows, staying up late. The memory of making s'mores with peanut butter cups instead of plain chocolate bars almost made her hungry.

Soon, she turned onto a beachfront road. The water was beautiful, sparkling and blue. A few other people were pulled off onto the side of the road so they could take a few photos or enjoy the scenery. She decided to stop too, pulling up in an empty spot and getting out.

The wind rustled her hair as she leaned against the side of her car. The beach here was always her favorite. Something about it made her feel like she was in a whole different world. She closed her eyes, inhaling the fresh sea air and savoring the gentle sounds of waves crashing against the sand and distant laughter from people playing with a frisbee closer to the water's edge.

After taking a few moments, she decided to head on; there would be plenty of time to enjoy the beach later. Charlotte started her car again and went to pull out, but she only heard one of her back wheels spinning. Giving the accelerator a harder tap didn't help either. She hopped out and went to look. A wheel was stuck in a sandy patch, so she couldn't get traction—she had pulled too far off the road.

Charlotte sighed and looked around, hoping to find a solution.

* * *

Briggs took in the latest small town on his meandering journey—Sea Breeze Cove. He had been staying in different small towns at B&Bs, resting for a day or two before moving on again. There was no rush since he didn't even have a destination. This town, though, stood out. He liked the look of it, and it wasn't just the bright sunshine and blue water that felt good for his soul.

Something about it was charming. Cape Cod style cottages lined the road, each one with beautiful landscaping and inviting colors out front. The town had similar buildings painted in soft nautical shades of blue and white, and tourists and locals walked along the sidewalks. Quaint was the word he was looking for. It felt like a place where people went to relax.

He kept driving through town and came out on the other side, turning onto a beachfront road. The sea was even more beautiful now that there were only a few dunes between him and the water. Fresh air streamed in through his open windows.

Up ahead, he saw a car struggling to pull off a soft patch on the side of the road, its wheel spinning and kicking up sand behind it. He pulled over in front of the car and got out, waving to the driver. She was beautiful, her auburn hair tousled from the wind in a way that made her seem carefree. But her face was scrunched in frustration as she tried to get the car to move, contrasting her hair.

"Need some help?" he asked.

"If it's not too much trouble," the woman replied, poking her head out the window.

"It's not. Give me a second to get something from my truck."

Briggs went to his truck and found something to put under the wheel to give it traction. He put it under the stuck wheel and went behind the car.

"I'll push while you accelerate," he called. The woman gave him a thumbs-up out the window.

He pushed the car as hard as he could, and it caught on the smooth surface he'd put down. The woman easily drove forward before pulling back onto the pavement.

"Thank you!" she said, looking back at him from the driver's side window. Her cheeks were flushed, and Briggs doubted it was from the sun.

"No problem."

He watched her drive away and went back to his truck, looking in the direction he had come from.

This might not be a bad place to stop for a while, he thought.

Charlotte's ears and cheeks burned a little on the rest of the drive to Jean's house. She couldn't believe she'd made such a silly mistake. Obviously she wasn't quite used to beach life, with sand everywhere and everything that came with it.

She was thankful that man had come along to help. It was hard to ignore how attractive he was, too, with his dark hair and striking blue eyes. His rugged looks weren't something she would easily find in Chicago. It went beyond his flannel shirt and worn jeans—it was just how he carried himself and exuded competence. Even though he hadn't said much, his actions had made a good impression.

Finally, she reached the cottage. It was close to the beach, so she parked carefully this time. Almost everything looked like she remembered it. The house was two stories high, with a little porch on the ground level. A big bay window and a small patio were on the second. There was also a guest house out back.

Charlotte found the key that the realtor who had

been handling the house left for her under the mat. She went inside, taking in all the details. The bones of the house were lovely, with spacious, high-ceilinged rooms and a picturesque view out back. Her bedroom was on the second floor, and had more than enough space for her.

But it wasn't quite as well-maintained as she'd hoped. Her aunt was so different from her mother, much more carefree and messy, and it showed in the house. There was peeling paint on both the outside and inside, plus dust in almost every room, and that wasn't even taking some bigger repairs into account. It was going to need some work to be truly livable.

Charlotte walked back downstairs, her stomach sinking a little. She hoped coming here wasn't a big mistake like her mom seemed to think it was.

CHAPTER FIVE

Despite the disarray of the cottage, Charlotte slept well, the sound of the waves in the distance soothing her. After getting dressed, she decided to head into town. She needed coffee first, so she went to the little coffee shop that she had passed on the way in, the same one her mother used to love frequenting.

There had been a lot of updates to the space. The walls were now painted a warm, sunshine yellow, but it still smelled like roasting coffee beans that tempted Charlotte from down the block. She passed some women having a coffee date on her way to the counter, where she ordered an iced latte and a blueberry muffin.

As she waited for her drink, she felt the man behind her in the line looking at her, almost as if he were trying to remember where he'd seen her before. Charlotte also tried to remember if she had seen him before. Had she known him as a child, or maybe he just happened to be someone she ran into all the time in Chicago, visiting the town?

"Excuse me—are you related to Jean?" the man asked.

"Yes, she was my aunt."

"Ah, I thought so." His eyes grew sad. "I'm so sorry for your loss. I'm Miles. I used to volunteer with Jean at the animal shelter."

"Thank you." Charlotte shook his hand, feeling touched by the stranger's kindness. "And nice to meet you. I'm Charlotte."

"Nice to meet you too, and welcome to town." He gave her a kind smile before taking his croissant and black coffee, heading out.

Charlotte got her coffee and started to leave, but some of the women she had passed when she came in stopped her. If she had to guess, she would have pegged them all to be around her age, in their early to mid-thirties.

One had blonde hair in a messy bun, sitting next to an adorable little girl who had to be her daughter, who was intensely focused on a coloring page of a unicorn. She had the same blonde hair as her mother, though her hair was up in pigtails.

One of the other women had reddish brown hair and a bright, energetic smile that was almost contagious. She seemed like the type of person who liked to be out and about, her skin glowing with a healthy tan and freckles. The last woman with ash brown hair and gray eyes had a quieter energy, but one Charlotte felt like she knew. Something about her reminded Charlotte of her old coworkers—smart and always willing to help.

"Hi, sorry to bother you. We just overheard that you're Jean's niece," the woman with blonde hair said. "Charlotte, right? We're sorry for your loss."

The other two women at the table echoed her sentiments.

"Thank you," Charlotte said, studying them curiously as she introduced herself. How had they known Jean if they were closer in age to her than to Jean? "All of you knew my aunt? Did you know her well?"

"We knew her, but not well. She volunteered at the shelter all the time," the woman with reddish brown hair said. "She tended to keep to herself. Or at least she kept to herself a lot more before her death.

She wasn't always like that. But she always loved the animals."

Charlotte nodded. They had to be talking about the shelter that Jean had left money to.

"Oh, I'm Addison, by the way, and this is my daughter Lainey," the blonde woman said, gently putting her hand on the little girl's head.

"And I'm Sadie," the one with reddish brown hair said.

"And I'm Elise," the final woman added with a smile. "Nice to meet you. Are you just in town to wrap up Jean's affairs?"

"No, I'm moving here for a while. I'll be living in Jean's old place," Charlotte said. "I need to spruce it up a bit, but I didn't want to let it go. It's such a lovely house with a lot of memories."

"I bet," Addison said. "Where did you move from?"

"Chicago. So this peace and quiet is a welcome change." Charlotte laughed. "I fell asleep without hearing a single siren or car horn honking."

"It's definitely peaceful around here!" Elise chuckled too. "Do you work from home, or do you have a job lined up here?"

"I'm actually on the lookout for one." Charlotte sipped her iced latte. "I used to work at a publisher back in Chicago, but they downsized my department."

"Ah, that stinks. I can keep an ear out for you," Sadie said. "And since you're new in town, do you want to join our book club? I'm assuming you like books if you worked in publishing."

"Yeah, it's low-key and meets every other week at the bookstore in town about three streets over," Elise added. "You should come by!"

"I'd love that! I'll definitely swing by."

Charlotte had been in book clubs before, but it had been a long time ago. It was the perfect place for her to meet new people, and she couldn't have been more grateful for the chance encounter.

* * *

Sadie drove away from her coffee date with her friends, feeling energized enough to take on her late morning dog walking clients. Her next dog was one of her favorites, though she had to admit it was hard to pick just one. Every single dog had something lovable about them, whether it was their loyalty, their sweet faces, or the weird little quirks that were unique to them. She had loved them since she was little, having grown up alongside a puppy her parents had gotten shortly before she was born.

Since she had a little extra time before she had to pick up the dog, she turned onto the longer route to her client's house, as she had done several times before.

She eventually stopped in front of a building with a "for lease" sign in the window, parking in the small lot and staring at the space longingly. It was the perfect space to expand her dog walking business into a doggy daycare and a boarding kennel. The location was on a road that connected the areas where a lot of her clients lived and the town center where many went to work.

The front window was a great spot for owners to see their dogs playing, and there was more than enough space for dogs to run around inside, and outside in the back grassy area. She only had to add a fence to make it safe back there. There was also plenty of room for boarders in the back. She couldn't have dreamed of a better spot.

But the thought of making such a huge change made her heart beat faster, and not in a good way. There were so many things associated with expanding a business that she got overwhelmed at the thought of even taking the first step. There was the business plan, securing funds, renovating the space, getting certain licenses, and hiring people. And all of that had to happen before it even opened.

She was confident in what she had at that moment: a dog walking business that she ran out of her home with a lot of loyal customers. Being able to get fresh air—at least when the weather was warm and clear—hang out with her favorite animals all day, and set her own hours was great. She couldn't have thought of a job more suited to her than this.

But a part of her wanted something bigger, a place that could solve a common problem her clients had. Sometimes just a walk or two in the middle of the day wasn't enough. Dogs got lonely just like humans, and creating a dog daycare could put owners at ease if they worried a lot.

Still, every time she Googled things like "scaling up your business" or "opening a new business location," she would panic a little. What if she couldn't handle renovations? What if she had read her clients' needs wrong and no one needed the day care? What if she couldn't manage employees? There were so many potential bad outcomes that Sadie couldn't keep out of her head.

She sighed and started her car up again, pulling

back onto the road. Her client's house wasn't far, and she used her key to open the backyard gate.

"Scout?" Sadie called.

The sweet, fluffy labradoodle's head popped up from where she was sleeping and she ran over to Sadie, almost bowling her over. Sadie laughed, kneeling down to scratch Scout behind her ears.

"Hi, buddy!" she cooed, moving her other hand to scratch Scout right above her tail. "Wow, you must be ready to burn off a little energy today. Ready to go for a walk?"

Scout danced in place, her tail whipping back and forth the moment she heard the word "walk". Sadie grinned as Scout rushed to grab her leash from the hook on the back of the door. Just like that, Sadie's mood brightened again.

Sea Breeze Cove's grocery stores were filled with all kinds of local produce, and Charlotte had taken advantage of the selection. The prices were much, much lower than the ones in Chicago, while the quality seemed to be much higher. Her bags were overflowing with juicy tomatoes, fragrant herbs, and fruit that looked so good that she was tempted to eat some before she even got home.

She groaned and bumped her car's back door closed with her hip, her arms weighed down by grocery bags. The first shopping trip after moving into a new place was always a big one, and as she always did, she tried to take everything in one go. Sure, making multiple trips was easier, but why not try to make it in one?

She started up the front stairs, humming with excitement, thinking of how she was going to curl up with a book and some freshly popped popcorn and wine, when her foot went straight through one of the wood steps. Letting out a little yelp, she managed to catch herself by balancing a hand on the box of wine she had bought. The steadiness didn't last long, since the wood on the next step up also buckled underneath her for a moment.

Thankfully she managed not to fall, but that didn't make her heart slow down at all.

Okay, that was way too close for my comfort, she thought.

The first thing on her to-do list was to start repairs on the house—it had definitely seen better days. It was a shame, being such a beautiful home. Charlotte wasn't sure what had made Jean neglect the house to such a degree, but she would have to fix it up if she was going to live there. Who knew what other pitfalls were waiting for her? If Jean had stepped through that stair when she was alive, she could have seriously injured herself.

Fixing up the house was something she could do in her aunt's memory too. Charlotte took a deep breath and continued inside without incident. Now that she'd had the close call, she noticed some rotting wood in other parts of the porch, plus a crack near the base of the wall that didn't seem like it was the result of anything good.

She was starting to get the sense that Jean didn't have the happiest life, and wished she had put more effort into getting to know her aunt. Just because her mother didn't get along with Jean, that shouldn't have kept Charlotte from reaching out. When she was younger, her mom could control whether she spoke to her aunt or not, and she had reason to follow her mom's lead. But as an adult, she didn't feel like she had an excuse.

Charlotte put her groceries away in the old fridge, then called Nina.

"Hey! How are things in Sea Breeze Cove?" Nina asked the moment she picked up.

"Not bad. It's so quiet here. I don't think I've

slept so hard in ages," Charlotte said, looking around for the chocolate-covered pretzels she had impulse bought. "And I met some nice women in the coffee shop who invited me to their book club."

"That's great! It sounds like things are off to a good start."

"They are. But I almost fell straight through the stairs on the front porch because the wood is rotted. Somehow I managed to catch myself before I fell." Charlotte found the pretzels and cradled her phone between her shoulder and ear to open the bag. "I need to get some serious help fixing things up. This isn't the kind of thing that's just a paint job and a heavy-duty clean away from being good to go."

"Yikes, I'm glad you're okay." Nina paused. "Why don't you put out a help wanted ad if there are that many repairs? The little town has to have a newspaper."

"I think it does. I'll do that as soon as I can. I'm not sure how much longer I can be here without something else breaking down."

CHAPTER SIX

Briggs stretched in the bed of his room at the Sea Breeze Cove B&B where he had been staying for a few nights, then got up to start his day early. He had to find somewhere a little more long-term if he was going to stay for a little bit. And a long-term place to live required work and an income to keep himself afloat.

Once he got dressed, he headed downstairs to the lobby of the B&B. As was the case at many of the B&Bs that he stayed in, the décor was warm, inviting, and slightly dated in a way that came across as charming. He much preferred them to bland hotel rooms. Moving around as much as he did made him appreciate small businesses and how unique they all were.

The owner was humming and tidying up, dusting and polishing a wood table until it shone again. She had been welcoming and more than willing to help out ever since he'd checked in, offering him extra pillows, desserts that she had left over from dinner, and tips for where to find the best seafood for a great price.

"Good morning, Tracey," Briggs said.

"Morning! Did you sleep well?" She put down the vase that she had been dusting.

"I did. I actually had a question for you—do you happen to know of any work in the area? I'm a handyman and can do just about anything most people need done around their homes."

"Hmm..." Tracey tucked her dust cloth into a bucket and swept her hands together. "A lot of the seasonal jobs have already been filled since the businesses here hire in the late spring, in preparation for the summer tourist season. You just missed the big hiring spree."

"Ah, shoot." Briggs ran a hand through his hair.

"But you can check the help wanted ads in the paper—there's bound to be something in there. Let me grab it from the kitchen."

Tracey disappeared into the kitchen and returned with the paper, handing it over.

"Thanks!" He opened it, searching for the help wanted section.

"Good luck!"

Briggs sat down and browsed it. Tracey was right —the job listings were sparse, mostly filled with office jobs, babysitting gigs, or tutoring jobs. His eyes fell on an ad requesting a handyman for renovations and repairs in a cottage. It definitely looked promising.

Charlotte was glad she had taken Nina's advice to put a help wanted ad in the local paper. In the days since the ad went up, she had gotten several repair men to look at the house and give her a quote. She anxiously watched the latest repairman, a middle-aged man with a bushy mustache wearing overalls, as he inspected a crack in the wall. He was hard to read, so she couldn't tell if he was going to give her some good or bad news.

"Alright, I think I've seen it all," the man said.

"How much do you think it'll be?" Charlotte asked. When he gave her his quote, she tried not to let her disappointment show. "I think that's a little out of my price range, but thank you for coming by."

"Not a problem. If you change your mind, here's

my card." The man dug into his pocket and handed her a card.

Once he left, she sighed. He was the latest of many repairmen to give her a quote that was out of her price range. She didn't have a ton of savings. Chicago was an expensive place to live, especially on a publishing salary. Plus, she had been the only one bringing in money since Peter was between jobs.

She still didn't have a job lined up in Sea Breeze Cove yet either. How was she going to manage this? The repairs had to be done, and soon. Part of her wanted to give up and go back home to her mom, admitting defeat, but she still had one more interview left.

Fifteen minutes later, there was another knock on the door. When she opened it, she was surprised to see the man who had helped her get her car out of the sand. He was just as good-looking up close as he had been at a distance, when helping her with her car. Maybe even more so. There were friendly smile lines around his eyes, though his expression was calm at the moment, and his eyes were a vivid blue.

"Uh, hi—are you Briggs Callahan?" Charlotte asked, trying to hide her surprise but failing.

"I am." He seemed surprised too, his blue eyes widening when he recognized her.

"Great, come in. I should thank you again for helping me with my car—now I'm a lot more cautious about where I park." Charlotte laughed, surprised at how nervous she sounded, but Briggs laughed too.

"It was no problem, seriously. But it was good timing, though. There are some potholes in the driveway and it looks like some sand has blown all the way over from the beach," he said, looking over his shoulder. "Are you interested in having those filled?"

"Sure, I suppose. My poor little car has been through a lot and I don't want to end up stuck in my own driveway."

"Alright, then." Briggs nodded and looked around. "Shouldn't be that hard since there are just a few."

They were still standing in the entryway of the house, which looked slightly better than the rest of it. The chandelier hanging from the high ceiling was dusty and covered in cobwebs, and half the lightbulbs didn't work, but it was easy to see how beautiful it must have been in its prime.

"Let me show you all the other things that need repairs." Charlotte stepped back so he would follow her further into the house. "You probably saw that stair and the porch when you came up."

"I did." He took the clipboard that he had tucked under his arm and pulled a pen from under the clip. "Does the porch wrap around to the back?"

"Not all the way around, but it runs the length of the house." Charlotte stepped over a stack of books. "Watch your step. I'm not sure what's happening with the floor here, but it's a little creaky and warped. Maybe water damage?"

Briggs nodded, gently pressing on the spot with his booted foot. It creaked, apparently in a way that told him something, and he scribbled something on his clipboard.

"It might have been a leak, or a recurring leak, definitely. Have you been here when it's been raining?" he asked.

"No, not yet. I've only been here for a little while. I was on my way into town for the first time in a while when you helped me out." Charlotte waited for him to nod, letting her know that he was ready to move on.

"Looking at that water stain on the ceiling, that might be because of it." Briggs stepped over a stack of books on the ground as they walked to the kitchen.

"The kitchen is pretty rough. I think there were

some leaks under the sink too." Charlotte winced. "I think the water might have attracted a few bugs."

Briggs didn't seem to mind. He opened up the cabinet and squatted down, pulling a flashlight off his belt loop. Again, Charlotte had no idea what he was looking for, but he seemed like he knew what he was doing. He stood up again, writing more things down. His dark eyebrows furrowed for a moment.

"Once that leak is fixed, you can call in an exterminator," he said. "Not much use calling them in now since bugs'll come back to water no matter what."

Charlotte nodded. Unfortunately she'd had more experience with bugs than she wanted to from various apartments she'd rented in Chicago.

She took Briggs through the other rooms on the first floor, which mostly had some chipped paint and a few cosmetic problems, then upstairs, which had some more plumbing issues and a few things that some of the other handymen hadn't noticed, like loose tiles on the wall and an odd noise coming from the toilet. Eventually she took him out back to show him the rest of the porch, then to the guest house.

The guest house looked like it hadn't been used in a while, but it was in better shape than the house. There was one bedroom and a bathroom, both with old wallpaper, and there were a few cracks in the wall that Briggs didn't seem worried about. It was livable, or at least it would be when Charlotte gave it a heavy dusting.

"That should be everything," Charlotte said, stopping on the back porch.

"Alright then, Here's your quote, plus a breakdown of what each thing costs," Briggs said, handing her the clipboard after writing a few more things down and pointing out the final number.

Charlotte's heart fell again when she took in the price. After a long day of interviews, this being the last one, it was hard to hide her disappointment. The itemized list of all the repairs made her head spin. Even if she was able to get a budget price on everything that Briggs had seen and pointed out, there was no way she could afford even the biggest projects.

"Thanks for coming out, but that's out of my price range," she said, handing him the clipboard again.

Briggs studied her face, thinking for a moment.

"Maybe I can help you out." He nodded toward the guest house. "Is there anyone living back there? Or planning to live back there in the near future?"

"No, it's empty and a little beat up, as you saw."

"I'm only in town for a short while and I need a place to stay. In exchange for letting me stay in the guest house, I could do all the work you need for free. All you'll have to cover is the cost of materials."

Charlotte perked up for a moment, but bit her lip. She was wary at first—even though he had helped her out on the side of the road and today, she didn't know him. But it was a good offer, and it wasn't like he was going to be staying in the house. Plus, she got a trustworthy vibe from him, though he was a little mysterious with his hint that he was just passing through town. She found herself curious about him, despite herself.

"Okay, let's do it," she said.

CHAPTER SEVEN

Charlotte watched Briggs back his truck up to the guest house the next day. When he told her he could move in right away she had been surprised, but apparently he traveled light just like she had. He didn't have a small trailer carrying his larger items—just whatever was in the back under a tarp.

"Need any help?" Charlotte asked as he stepped out of his truck.

"No, I'm good. I don't have that much." He pulled the tarp off of the pickup, revealing all of his tools, a few little appliances, and some other things she couldn't make out from where she was standing, but that was it. "But thanks!"

"No problem. I'll be inside if you need me."

She headed inside, finished up her coffee and waited for him to come in and start his work.

"All moved in," he said, poking his head through the open front door. "I'm ready to start on the house."

"Great!" Charlotte smiled. "Will you need a lot of space around here, or can I sort through some stuff while you work?"

"You can sort things out. I was going to start in the kitchen to shore up the leaks so you can get an exterminator in," he said, coming all the way inside. He was dressed just as she expected a handyman would be, in a lightweight flannel shirt, work pants, and boots.

"Okay, thanks. Let me know if you need anything—I'll just be over here." Charlotte gestured to the living room, which had a view straight into the kitchen.

Briggs just gave her a nod and put his tool kit down next to the sink. Charlotte tied her hair up into a tighter bun, then looked around at the disarray in front of her. There were so many little knickknacks, books, mugs, and more that Charlotte hardly knew where to start. Plus, everything was covered in dust.

She sighed, and decided to dust first. Then she

would tackle the clutter in sections based on how frequently she would use each area.

First came the things that lined the walls, like old books and decorative pieces that narrowed the pathway a little bit. She kneeled down and started going through the books, trying not to get distracted by reading them. Soon the stack of books to donate grew taller and taller, as did the cluster of knickknacks that she wanted to get rid of.

As she worked throughout the morning, she peeked into the kitchen from time to time, watching Briggs work. He was fiddling with a wrench and looking inside, a slight furrow of concentration in his brow. Feeling like she was staring at him, she went back to work, moving on to another section of the room. There was so much to go through—the house had pretty much been left as it was on the day Jean had passed.

She kept waiting for Briggs to come ask her a question or, when she got to the side of the room where she was close enough to talk with him, to start making small talk. But he kept working in silence, not even listening to music. She didn't want to bother him anyway, as curious as she was about him. Plus, she needed to get through all of Jean's stuff.

* * *

Briggs sat back on his heels, looking under the sink for a moment before glancing at Charlotte in the living room. She was moving a big stack of books, blowing a lock of auburn hair that had escaped from her ponytail away from her face. He was curious about her. From what he'd noticed when he'd helped her move her car, she was from out of state—Illinois, if he remembered correctly. And she'd mentioned that she had been coming back for the first time in a while.

But this house seemed to be hers if she was hiring him to fix it up. Yet, it didn't seem like any of the things in the house were hers, besides some items in the bathroom and the brightly colored bedspread in the master bedroom that sharply contrasted with the dull paint on the walls. It seemed like an older person's home that had fallen into disrepair.

He double-checked his work under the sink, which was a simple fix. There was just a loosened bolt on the pipe, plus a small crack that he sealed. He found some fresh cabinet liners that he had left over from a job back in Bangor and replaced the water-stained one. Once he finished, he got up and turned the tap on, still watching Charlotte out of the corner of his eye.

He wanted to ask her what had brought her here. Was this a family home that she inherited? Or had she bought it, sight unseen? The latter didn't make sense—if she bought the house to flip it, she would have had more of a budget for repairs.

Something about the way she moved, sometimes murmuring to herself and frowning at stacks of stuff, her hands on her hips, made her seem out of her element. He couldn't quite pin her down with what he knew about her. She was a bit younger than him, though not by that much, and had a nice bookish energy. From what he could tell, she had been focusing on the books almost exclusively, standing there and flipping through them thoroughly before putting them aside.

Maybe she had come here to escape, just like he had. But why did she want a fresh start? He usually didn't tell people his story, so asking her about why she was there wasn't fair. That didn't stop him from being curious, though.

Elise weaved her way through the kitchen of her father's restaurant, Firefly Bistro, trying to avoid getting run over by a chef or a waiter. Warm, familiar smells washed over her, like her father's incredible red sauce and the roasted chicken that put all other chicken to shame. The beginning of the dinner rush was always chaotic, and trying to find him in it all was surprisingly difficult.

She found him at the entry to the kitchen, looking over tickets with a frown on his face while people came up to him asking questions. He threw his hand holding the tickets in the air and sighed once he was finally left alone, sliding a few tickets into the slot for the chef to look over.

It wasn't an unusual sight. Elise almost considered the restaurant a sibling since her dad loved it so much and he had run it since she was small. He could manage the constant chaos and stress of running it well when he was younger, but he was approaching retirement age. She could see how much it wore on him in the lines in his face and the way his hair was graying faster than ever.

"Dad, you've got to hire someone to help you out. You're trying to be an octopus back here," Elise said, putting a hand on her father's back. "You can't be everywhere and do everything at once.

"It's fine. It's just busy, and busy is good, isn't it? I've been running this place since you were a little one and I can handle it myself."

"You can, huh?" Elise raised an eyebrow and gestured at the tickets in front of him. "So these tickets, the piles of receipts in the back, the order forms... they're all things you can handle?"

His office was far worse than that, but she didn't want to lay it on too thick. It looked as if a paper mill had exploded next to a coffee shop between all the empty cups from the place down the street and the records he still insisted on keeping in hard copy instead of digital. The scanner that Elise had gotten him was collecting dust somewhere under all of the piles.

He wasn't the type of person to eschew technology all together—he liked his smartphone—but for some reason, he clung to his paper for the restaurant. If she looked, she knew she'd find receipts from meals that Firefly Bistro had served when she was a teenager.

"Well, yeah, I can handle it." He paused. "Eventually. It's just a sign that things are going well."

Elise sighed. He had a point. The restaurant's business was still booming and had become a mainstay in Sea Breeze Cove. The fact that he had sustained the business at such a high level for so many years was admirable, but he had to slow down at some point.

He was so stubborn and hardworking that he thought he could do anything if he tried hard enough. But even he had limits, and Elise was worried that he was going to fly over that edge without warning.

"I know, I know. I just worry," Elise said.

"I know you do. You've got your heart in the right place," Arthur said, looking behind him at the clock. "Don't you have to be somewhere?"

"Yeah, I do." Elise sighed again.

"I'll be fine, I promise. Go and have fun."

Elise gave him a kiss on the cheek and headed out, saying hello to the host. Tonight was her book club at the local bookstore, The Book Nook, and she didn't want to miss it. The bookstore was small, but it made up for its size in character. It was bright and warm, the walls stuffed to the gills with bookshelves painted in bright colors.

The owner, Daisy, had carried a flower theme throughout, and included hanging planters and fresh flowers on any surface that wasn't filled with a book. If Elise had to conjure up an image of a bookstore owner, Daisy would fit the bill perfectly. Her enthusiasm for reading and books was evident in almost every interaction, and she had a book recommendation for everyone and anyone, even if they claimed they weren't readers. She put the same energy into the book club.

In the time since Elise had been going to book club, her reading horizons had expanded significantly. Her small bookcase was overflowing with paperbacks and hardcovers in all sorts of genres. Plus, the other ladies in the club made reading a group activity. She couldn't wait to talk about how she felt about this session's book.

"Hey, Elise!" Daisy greeted as Elise walked toward the stairs in the back of the store. "Here for book club?"

"Yep!" Elise held up her book, a fast-paced psychological thriller. "It was a great one."

"I absolutely adored it. See you up there in a bit!"

Elise headed upstairs to the meeting area, where book club was always held. It was the same size as the shop downstairs but without the bookshelves, it felt big. Sometimes there were book signings and launch events in the space too. Elise's two friends Sadie and Addison were already there, plus around a half-dozen other women. Elise, Sadie and Addison were on the younger end of the group, with the oldest women probably in their fifties.

"Hey, guys," Elise said, plopping into a chair next to Sadie. "How's it going?"

"Not too bad," Sadie said, thumbing through the book. "I just finished the book last night so everything's really fresh in my head."

"I always start and finish too early." Addison smoothed her hand over the cover of her book. "Everyone's going to have to jog my memory. At least I know I liked it and there were so many twists that I could hardly keep up."

"That's pretty much what we talk about the whole time anyway—how much we loved or hated it." Elise laughed.

"True," Addison said. "Sometimes I don't understand how I could forget some of the details that everyone remembers. My memory's not *that* bad."

"You have a very energetic five year old who likes to wake up at the crack of dawn every morning—I'm surprised you're up and alert some days." Sadie smiled.

"Okay, true." Addison shook her head. "And most of the time, we're re-reading her favorite books or watching her favorite movies over and over again. If you asked me to recite the entirety of Beauty and the Beast, I'd have you covered."

They all laughed. Elise babysat from time to time and had seen Beauty and the Beast what felt like ten thousand times as a result.

The room continued to fill with a few more people, and then with Daisy, who sat in her usual seat opposite the door.

Charlotte appeared in the doorway not long after, peeking inside as if she wasn't sure she was in the right place. Elise waved and smiled, taking her purse off of the seat next to her.

"Hey, you made it!" Elise said.

"It's good to see you again," Sadie added, Addison nodding in agreement.

"It's nice to see you all again too." Charlotte's nerves seemed to slip away as she sat down and pulled out her book. "I'm glad this book was a page-turner. I ripped through it in a lazy afternoon."

"Same here." Elise looked around at everyone, spotting Daisy looking at Charlotte with a curious look. "Oh, let me introduce you to people—this is Daisy, who owns the store."

Charlotte and Elise stood so they could go shake Daisy's hand.

"Nice to meet you!" Charlotte said. "This is such an adorable bookstore."

"Thank you!" Daisy smiled. "It's small but mighty."

"Charlotte just moved here from Chicago. She used to work in publishing, too," Elise said.

"Wow, how interesting! So of course you're right at home in a bookstore." Daisy laughed.

"Bookstores are definitely a home away from home. I miss the indie ones I used to go to back in Chicago."

Elise looked to Charlotte, and asked, "If I'm not mistaken, you're still on the hunt for a job, right?"

Charlotte nodded. Elise hoped that Daisy would bite on the offer of help. The Book Nook was small but busy, and having someone who could help her out would take a lot off of Daisy's shoulders. Just like her father, she had run her business on her own the entire time it had been open and she was getting up in years. It couldn't have been easy for her to keep up. If she couldn't get her father to hire someone else, perhaps she could help Daisy get the help she needed.

"What perfect timing—I've been looking for some more help here." Daisy's smile turned relieved. "Can you come in for an interview tomorrow? I can tell you more about what I'm looking for."

"That would be great!" Charlotte perked up again, and Elise smiled.

"Perfect! Remind me to grab your phone number just in case after the meeting." Daisy checked her watch. "We have to get started."

Charlotte and Elise took their seats again as Daisy started the meeting, both of them still smiling at the serendipitous timing.

CHAPTER EIGHT

Charlotte left the book club feeling more energized than she had in a while despite the late hour. She had been on the fence about going earlier—she was tired after a long day of cleaning and honestly, a little anxious about meeting new people. Making friends as an adult was hard, even when people invited you places. She felt out of practice, almost. Most of the people she had met in the recent past were friends of friends or coworkers.

But she was glad she'd made the effort. The book was an amazing choice—fast-paced, smart, and well-written. Charlotte had heard of the author, but she hadn't had the chance to pick up anything by him yet. Now she had at least five books in the author's backlist to enjoy.

And everyone in the group was fun, too. There were certain plot points that were polarizing, and everyone animatedly argued for their point of view, offering insights that Charlotte was still turning over in her head. It was just the kind of thing she needed in her life, especially now that she was in a new place.

And even better, she had a job interview at The Book Nook the next day. She had worked in bookstores in college, from big ones like Barnes and Noble to small indies, and she vastly preferred the indie stores. Being able to form relationships with customers and hand-sell books always came naturally to her. Plus, she already liked Daisy. It was a perfect match, or so she hoped.

Charlotte adjusted her headlights. The coastal roads didn't have street lamps, so she took extra care to not speed or get distracted. After getting stuck in the sand her first day, she wanted to avoid mishaps at all costs.

But as she adjusted her lights, they illuminated something lying in the street. She slammed the brakes and swerved a little around it, coming to a stop and putting her hazard lights on, just in case. Her heart was pounding so hard that she pressed her hand to her chest as if she could slow it down.

When she looked out to see what she almost hit, she realized it was a dog. Its fur was dark with some patches of brown, but she couldn't tell what breed he was. All she knew was that the dog was hurt.

* * *

Briggs finished brushing his teeth and headed into the small kitchen of the guest house to grab a glass of water. The guest house was just the right size for him, though it also needed work like the rest of the house. He had taken care of a leak in the bathroom that thankfully hadn't damaged anything, and aside from that, he'd put the guest house projects on the backburner. Sure, he didn't love the old floral wallpaper or the Formica countertop in the kitchenette, but there were much more pressing things waiting for him.

He put his glass down and picked up a photo he always kept by his bedside—his late wife and son. They were at the beach, grinning and posing next to a haphazard sandcastle that they had spent ages making. Briggs still remembered that day clearly. The smell of the ocean, their loud laughter, the way his wife's brown eyes had looked across the big fire they had built.

As he did every night, he kissed his fingers, then pressed them to the picture before putting the photo away. He couldn't fall asleep without doing it.

He slid under the covers and clicked off the lamp, but the moment he got comfortable, there was a knock at the front door. His brows pulled together. What could someone want at this hour?

He got up and answered the door, finding Charlotte standing there. Her skin was pale and she was wringing her trembling hands. There was a bit of blood on her sleeve too, which replaced the last bits of sleepiness in his head with worry.

"Sorry for bothering you so late," she said, her breathing a little heavy. "But I need your help."

* * *

Charlotte felt bad about bugging Briggs. He had clearly been in bed, possibly even asleep from the way his hair was sticking up in the back. He had already helped her more times than she liked. But in this case, the help was definitely needed. She had barely managed to get the dog in her car, and she worried that she would hurt it more if she tried to get it out on her own. The dog was light, definitely on the skinny side, but she had no idea if it had internal injuries she couldn't see.

"Here it is," Charlotte said, opening the door to her backseat. "Can you help me get it out?"

"Ah, jeez." Brigg's eyes softened. "Of course I can."

He gently picked the dog up. While Charlotte was upset that it was hurt, she was glad that the dog was gentle, even though it was in pain. Charlotte walked ahead of them and inside the house, thankful that Jean had a collection of old blankets. She made a makeshift bed of them in the kitchen since that was where she'd stored some first-aid supplies.

Briggs put the dog down as gently as he could, but it still whimpered a little. It rested its head on the blankets, panting slightly and closing its eyes. Now that she was seeing the dog in the light, Charlotte could tell that it was a mutt of some kind, almost like a Rottweiler in its coloring and marking, but smaller and a bit fluffy aside from the nasty scrape on its side. Some of its fur was matted, but it didn't look as if it had lived on the street for its entire life.

"I don't know the first thing about dog first-aid," Charlotte said, grabbing the kit. "But it should be similar, right?"

"Do you have your phone? Maybe you could

look it up while I see what we have." Briggs took the kit from her and opened it. "I know the basics, but I'm not sure if those apply to dogs either."

"Good idea." Charlotte found her phone and quickly looked up first-aid tips for dogs.

"I'm glad we looked this up—it seems like we'll have to patch him up with water and clean bandages, no alcohol or hydrogen peroxide," Charlotte said, grabbing the kit again. "Let's clean up this scrape first."

Briggs gently petted the dog's neck, which didn't have a collar on it. "I think his back leg might be broken too."

"Yeah, it doesn't look good." Charlotte dampened a cloth and dabbed at the wound to clean it. The dog whimpered and Briggs held him in place where he could so Charlotte could finish. Right away, Charlotte could tell that the dog felt comfortable with them, even though he had every reason not to trust humans.

"Do you see anything else that's wrong?" Charlotte asked quietly.

Briggs checked over the dog. "I don't think so. Do you?"

Charlotte sighed, biting her bottom lip and

dabbing the scrape dry. "I don't think so either, but I'll have to call the vet."

"Yeah, this seems like it's out of our paygrade." Briggs studied the dog for a few moments. "He looks a little skinny, doesn't he?"

"A bit. I'd bet he's hungry. Maybe that would help him heal a little more?" Charlotte looked at Briggs, then looked at the dog again.

"Let me see if he'll eat something. Be right back," Briggs said, getting up.

Charlotte sat next to the patient, gently petting his head as she pulled out her phone. After a quick search, she found the number for the local vet's office. She got a recorded message right away, telling her it was closed, but would reopen tomorrow morning.

"They don't open until tomorrow," Charlotte said when Briggs returned with some sliced ham.

Briggs knelt down near the dog, whose nostrils flared as his eyes opened again. Still, he stayed on his side, not lifting his head. Charlotte's heart rate picked up a little. Was he too injured to eat or drink?

"C'mon, buddy," Briggs said softly, offering the dog some rolled-up ham. "It'll be good for you."

The dog gently took the ham from his hands,

eating it before resting his head again. Both of them let out a sigh of relief.

"That's better than nothing, I suppose. At least for now." Charlotte tried to offer the dog more ham, but didn't succeed in getting him to take it.

"I'll help you get him to the vet tomorrow morning," Briggs said.

"You really don't have to," Charlotte said. "That's not in your job description."

Briggs grinned. "I'm the handyman—that could mean a lot of things. Why not dog care?"

CHAPTER NINE

Charlotte's eyes flew open early the next morning after a night of restless sleep. She hadn't been able to stop thinking about the dog, so she rushed downstairs to check on him.

The dog was still where they'd left him, panting a little on his bed of blankets. Charlotte checked the time. The vet's office was going to open soon and she wanted to take him in right away, but it was still so early. She wasn't sure if she should disturb Briggs at this hour, especially since he was already going out of his way to help her.

She sighed and scratched the dog behind his ears, making him give her a weak twitch of his tail. When she stood, the answer to her problem was solved. Briggs was coming toward the cottage, checking his watch and looking back at the building as if he too was debating whether to knock on her door.

Charlotte rushed over and opened the door, waving at him.

"Hey, good morning," she said. "Come on in."

"Morning."

Briggs came in and made a beeline to the dog, who also twitched his tail when Briggs petted its neck.

"How'd he hold up last night?" Briggs asked.

"He was quiet—not even a whine or a bark. I could hardly sleep worrying about him, though. I figured that moving him upstairs to the bedroom, then back down wouldn't be good for him." Charlotte rested her hands on her hips. "I was just about to get dressed to take him to the vet."

"Okay, I'll stay down here with him."

"Thank you."

Charlotte ran upstairs to change, then came back down with her car keys in hand. Just as he had the night before, Briggs gently picked up the dog and cradled him in the blankets. They went out to the car and Charlotte watched him put the dog in the backseat.

She opened her mouth to ask him if he could

come too, just to keep the dog stable, but he walked around to the other side and got into the backseat with the dog. Problem solved again. She got into the car and started it up, glancing in her rearview mirror to back out and catching Briggs as he continued petting the dog, murmuring something soothing.

She pulled out slowly so as to not jostle their passenger, checking her rearview mirror again. Briggs was still talking to the dog. He was leaning in as if he were sharing a secret, his blue eyes gentle and kind. Whatever he was saying was too quiet to hear, but the sight of them warmed her heart anyway.

"Morning, Pearl," Ethan said to his secretary at the small vet clinic he ran. "Do we have anything on the schedule for this morning?"

"Nope! Not a single dog or cat or critter is due in until later this morning," Pearl replied.

"Great. I'll be in my office until then." Ethan smiled and slipped into his office.

Ethan rarely had a slow start to the morning, so he was going to use it as well as he could. Though the vet clinic was small, he still had a lot of patients to prepare for.

Humming to himself, he opened up the digital chart for a sassy Yorkshire terrier that he was going to see a little later. The dog had some dental issues that they had been working to clear up for a while. One of his favorite parts of his job was seeing an animal's health gradually get better. There was no hiding a dog's feelings when they felt better, and that brightened Ethan's day every time.

Just when he got into the chart, Pearl poked her head into his office.

"Sorry to bother you, but we have a walk-in with an injured dog," Pearl said, glancing over her shoulder again with worry in her eyes.

"Send them into the exam room. I'll be there in a moment."

Ethan closed out what he was doing and went into the exam room, finding an attractive woman with auburn hair and a man with dark hair. He didn't recognize either of them, but he had seen expressions like theirs time and time again in his clinic—worry and fear.

They weren't touching, but something about the way they stood next to each other suggested that there was something between them. Ethan glanced at their hands—neither of them were married. Maybe they were just dating.

"Hello, I'm Dr. Gilbert," Ethan said, taking a look at the dog on the examination table. "And what's this dog's name? Are you both his owners?"

"Oh, we're not together. Not like that." The woman's cheeks flushed pink. "He's doing work on my house and..."

She trailed off, as if she realized that explaining how they'd both come to the clinic wasn't a priority.

"I'm Charlotte, and this is Briggs," the woman continued. "The dog isn't ours—I found it on the road last night with that scrape. And I think it has a broken leg too."

* * *

Charlotte was sure that her cheeks were still a little red even though they had moved past the introductions already.

Why did I blush so hard when the vet assumed we were together? Pull it together, Charlotte, she thought, swallowing and trying to shake off her embarrassment. *It's not a big deal.*

Maybe she'd blushed as hard as she had because she knew that she found Briggs attractive. It was hard for her to not notice him when she saw him every day. But it was just that—she thought he was handsome and a great handyman, not to mention good with dogs.

Dr. Gilbert ran his fingers along the dog, quietly apologizing to him when he prodded a sore spot that made him whine. The vet looked young, probably in his mid-thirties, but he examined the dog in a practiced way.

"Yeah, that leg definitely looks broken. He'll need a few stitches for this scrape since the wounds are a little deep, and a cast for his leg," Dr. Gilbert said, feeling the dog's back near his head. "And since he's a stray, I can do bloodwork to make sure he doesn't have any other conditions. I don't feel a microchip."

"Thank you. Sounds great," Charlotte said. She was incredibly grateful that she had bartered with Briggs so she could use some of her savings on the vet bills.

"I'll get him in his cast, if you'd like to wait in the waiting room."

Charlotte and Briggs did as the doctor said and headed into the waiting room, sitting down in the hard plastic seats.

"Thanks again for helping me out," Charlotte said. "I'm glad the dog will be okay."

"Yeah, no problem." Briggs smiled a little. "He

seems like a good dog. I can't believe he was that calm even though he was in pain."

"Yeah. When I first picked him up I was afraid he'd fight me. Poor thing was probably hurting too much." Charlotte ran her fingers through the end of her ponytail. "Hopefully he'll get some meds to ease the pain."

"I bet he will. It seems like Dr. Gilbert has everything well under control."

"I'll try to find out who the dog belongs to next, I guess." Charlotte shrugged, looking at a poster of a dog eating some vet-approved food in front of her. "It seems like he's been on the streets for a little while. Or he rolled in some mud at some point."

"He probably doesn't belong to anyone. Well, maybe he did a long time ago, but it seems like he's been without a home for a long time." Briggs rested his ankle across his knee. "What will you do if you can't find an owner for him?"

Charlotte paused, thinking for a few moments. "I'm not sure. I've always wanted a dog, but my mom thought they shed too much and were too messy. One of my best friends growing up had one. My mom once saw the dog roll in the dirt in the back, then go sprinting through the house and all over the white carpet...that pretty much killed any hopes I had of getting a dog."

They both laughed.

"I bet," Briggs said.

"It's like the dog knew right where to run. I think that was the only room with white carpet." Charlotte shook her head. "I've always wondered why dogs do that thing where they run around like crazy when they get inside. Especially if they were just outside, where there's so much more room to run!"

"Those little quirks are half the fun." Briggs smiled gently. "My old dog used to love playing with..."

He stopped, his posture tensing ever so slightly and the smile dropped from his eyes, but not his mouth. So he'd had a dog in the past, and from the gentle tone he shifted to when talking about him, the dog was well-loved. And for whatever reason, he didn't want to talk about something as simple as a past pet. Charlotte didn't want to press him since she was sure he had his reasons, but he had piqued her curiosity.

CHAPTER TEN

"You good, buddy?" Charlotte asked the dog, who was sitting on his stack of blankets near a window.

He had a nice view of the beach in the distance, with birds flocking on the patch of grass that ran up against the sand. With his cast, he was able to hobble, but not run, but Charlotte had the feeling that he was going to be chasing seagulls in the near future. His ears always perked up when one flew into view.

The dog thumped his tail a few times, making Charlotte smile. He had all the pain medication he needed, plus that good view. Dr. Gilbert had said he'd probably sleep most of the day anyway, which was perfect since he had to be alone for a little while. Charlotte gave him a few scratches on the head before heading into town.

In her rush out the door that morning to take the dog to the vet, she hadn't had any coffee, so first she headed to the cafe she had been to before. She got an iced latte again, and as she waited for her drink, she saw the older gentleman who'd introduced himself as Miles come into the shop.

"Hey, Charlotte!" Miles smiled. "Funny running into you again."

"Hi, Miles! It's nice to see you again." Charlotte perked up as she recalled what he had told her about being a volunteer at the local animal shelter. "And it's great timing, actually. Has anyone reported a dog missing to the shelter? I found a dog last night on the road."

"Hm, not that I can recall." Miles furrowed his brow. "What's he look like?"

Charlotte pulled up the picture that she had taken of the dog late yesterday. He already looked much, much better now that he had more food in him and he had been brushed.

"Oh, poor thing. Broken leg?" Miles asked, handing Charlotte her phone again.

"Yeah. Luckily it was just that and those scrapes." Charlotte tucked her phone into her purse again.

"I can't fathom how someone could hit an

innocent dog and keep driving." Miles shook his head.

"I know." Charlotte shook her head too. "He's very sweet, so it seems like he must have had an owner at some point. But as you saw, he's a little on the thin side, so it must have been a while."

"I bet. I haven't seen anyone looking for a dog like that in a long time, unfortunately," Miles said, making Charlotte deflate. "But if you send me that picture, I can post it at the shelter if anyone comes looking."

"That would be perfect, thank you!"

Miles gave her his email address and Charlotte continued on her walk through town to the bookstore. Her memories were slowly coming back, and she could easily navigate town based on a few long-standing landmarks that had been there since she was a teenager. She took a deep breath, steeling herself for the interview as she passed by shop after shop.

Daisy hadn't given her many details to go off of besides the fact that she needed help from someone who knew about the book business. Charlotte definitely had that experience. But what was Daisy looking for specifically? Did she need help with the financials, which Charlotte could handle but didn't love? Or simple things like inventory and running the cash register?

At least she had met Daisy and knew she was great boss material.

"Hey, thanks for coming in!" Daisy greeted when Charlotte walked inside. "Come on back to the office."

Charlotte followed her into a back room, which was stuffed with a desk and other boxes of books. The boxes came up to Charlotte's hip and she had to awkwardly maneuver around them to the chair. Daisy laughed, putting a stack of books to the side of her desk so she could see Charlotte clearly.

"Sorry, I swear I have my act together." Daisy moved more books so Charlotte had more leg room. "It's just that I've had a lot of things on my to-do list and I can't quite get the shelving done. But that's why we're here!"

Charlotte sat and handed Daisy her resume, butterflies fluttering in her stomach. Daisy studied her resume, nodding and slowly starting to smile.

"Great, thank you for this," Daisy said, putting Charlotte's resume down. "Your publishing experience is really great. Just from reading this I can tell you know your way around the book business."

"Thank you." Charlotte's cheeks flushed.

"Working at a small publisher really helped me get a sense of the different aspects of selling a book. And working at bookstores did too, of course."

"Definitely." Daisy nodded. "I should probably explain what the job will be. As you can see, this shop isn't very big, so there won't be much of a chance for you to use all of your skills—you'll mostly be maintaining stock and dealing with customers."

"That's fine with me. If I get the chance to talk to someone about books, I'm down to do it."

"That's fantastic." Daisy's smile broadened. And I see you have marketing experience, including digital marketing. I'm not too proud to admit that I have absolutely no idea what any of that involves, but I know I need it. Could you help out with that too? Do you have any ideas right off the bat?"

"I can help with that. I don't know how to make a website or anything, but I could figure out who to hire to do that. And I'm pretty good at social media. Instagram would be great for the shop since we could take pictures of new arrivals and post nice graphics of our event calendar." Charlotte paused for a moment, thinking of more things to accomplish. "Oh! And maybe we could set up a way to buy or reserve signed editions online. And I think the front window could definitely be utilized more..."

Daisy grinned, holding up a hand. "Okay, wonderful! All of that sounds fantastic and much beyond my knowledge base. Can you work all the days we're open?"

"Yep! My schedule is flexible." Cleaning the house could wait, and she trusted Briggs to work in the house when she wasn't around.

"Perfect." Daisy folded her hands on the desk. "There are ebbs and flows of customers, just like any place, but we have weekly events that you can see on the calendar near the door—book club, of course, YA book club, story time, and some author events."

Charlotte nodded—she had taken a good look at the calendar and had filed away several events for later.

"I've been super overwhelmed lately just doing day to day things, so I'm finally going to take Elise's advice and get some help. She's been hounding me about it every single book club for weeks." Daisy shook her head. "She's such a worrier, but I don't mind it. She's just trying to look out for the people she cares about, you know?"

"Yeah. It's a nice trait to have in a friend."

"I totally agree. And I'll have to thank her for introducing you to me." Daisy extended her hand to Charlotte. "You've got the job."

* * *

Charlotte grunted as she moved a stack of surprisingly heavy magazines that had been piled up in a corner of the living room. Once she put it down, she sighed and looked around. There was a ton of clutter—lots of knickknacks that Jean must have purchased on a whim without knowing where to put them, old magazines, binders, and more.

A lot of it was interesting, though, like Jean's collection of old copies of National Geographic and her embroidery projects. To Charlotte's surprise, her "keep" pile was growing more and more the deeper she dug.

There were a lot of decorative gems, though some things were pretty eccentric. The abstract paintings she had found, some of which were hidden behind furniture, were going to look great in the bedroom. She laughed, picking up a painting that definitely wasn't going to go on the walls, or anywhere—it looked like someone had tried to imitate Picasso and failed miserably.

She wanted to find the balance between keeping her aunt's memory alive and making the place her own. For now, she was going to use Jean's art, but eventually she would add more of her touch.

Charlotte stepped over a box of cat figurines and heard Briggs drilling something downstairs in the kitchen. At least if she got buried under a pile of stuff, she could easily call someone for help. Her next goal was to clear out and organize a box of papers. Jean had a lot of them, and from what Charlotte had seen, many of them weren't at all necessary.

She settled on the couch, the box next to her, and started to pull out pieces. She stacked the papers she was going to toss out next to her, and the ones that she was going to keep on the table in front of her. The "toss" pile was so big that it almost toppled over, but eventually she came across something that made her pause.

It was a packet of letters addressed to her mom, Melissa, all stamped but clearly unsent. Charlotte held them for a few moments before putting them in the keep pile, just in case her mom wanted them. They almost never spoke when Jean was alive, so Charlotte wasn't sure. *Better to check than to toss something valuable*, she thought.

Charlotte finished going through the box and stretched. It was well past time for a break, so she headed downstairs.

"Hey, pup," Charlotte said when she saw the dog

across the living room, lying on his bed on the floor next to the window. The dog looked up at her and wagged his tail.

Dr. Gilbert had given the dog a clean bill of health—everything was great besides the injuries from where he'd gotten hit by the car.

The dog whined a little, which Charlotte completely understood. His broken bone probably still hurt quite a bit even though he'd been at Charlotte's for several days now. She headed into the kitchen and bumped into Briggs, who was holding the bottle of pills containing the dog's meds.

"Ah, I guess we had the same idea. I was going to give him his meds, plus some food and water," Charlotte said.

"I'll bring him the pills if you bring the food and water." Briggs gently shook the pill bottle.

Charlotte filled up the dog's bowls and headed into the living room, putting them down in front of him so he didn't have to get up. He dug right in, taking his medicine after Briggs slipped it into his food.

Charlotte gently petted the back of his neck as he wolfed down his food.

"It's funny how we take so much care to perfectly formulate dog food with all the nutrients they need, but humans just eat whatever," Briggs said.

Charlotte nodded, then grinned when the dog buried his face deep into the food bowl.

"Delicious, huh, buddy?" Charlotte said with a chuckle. "To each their own, I guess. I can't imagine being excited about food pellets."

"Me either." Briggs looked down at the dog with a gentle smile on his face. "It doesn't smell great and doesn't look that exciting either."

"I don't think dogs have the most discriminating taste, though. I caught him trying to eat a paper bag with a ketchup stain on it on the beach yesterday."

Briggs laughed. "Okay, fair point. If we let them have full reign..."

"It would be like letting a toddler run wild in the candy aisle."

"Exactly."

They watched the dog eat for a little while. He hadn't gained a lot of weight yet, but if he continued to eat like this, it was only a matter of time.

"You need to give him a name," Briggs said, crouching down to pet the dog closer to his tail. "Even if you don't keep him. Calling him 'pup' or 'buddy' isn't really a name."

"Agreed." Charlotte nodded. "But what should it be?"

She waited for the dog to take a break from his eating and looked at him. He had the sweetest brown eyes, and sometimes he almost looked like he was smiling at everything.

"Hm...how about Bruno? It was the first thing that came to mind," Charlotte said. The dog perked up, wagging his tail, and licked her face, making Charlotte smile. "You like that, huh?"

"Bruno it is." Briggs grinned and gave Bruno a scratch in one of his favorite spots.

CHAPTER ELEVEN

Charlotte gave herself one more look in her rearview mirror before getting out of her car. It was her first day of work at the bookstore, and admittedly, she was a bit nervous. Even though she felt qualified, it was hard to shake those first day jitters, no matter how often she started somewhere new.

Before she could spend any more time hesitating, she got out of the car and walked down the block to the store.

"Good morning!" Daisy said the moment Charlotte walked in. "I'm so glad you're here!"

"I'm glad to be here too!" Charlotte smiled.

"Let me give you the lay of this small piece of land on the way to the back, where you can put your purse." Daisy waved her along as she walked toward the office.

The fiction section was right up front, with bestsellers prominently displayed on a table. There was also a display of authors who lived in the region too. It was well-organized by genre, so it wouldn't be hard for Charlotte to find anything someone might want.

The non-fiction section was a little smaller, just because Daisy knew more people came in for fiction at her store, but it was still very robust with bestsellers and little-known, but well-received books sprinkled in. The children's section rounded everything out, with picture books and learning toys on one side of the section and young adult fiction on the other.

Charlotte put her bag down in the back and Daisy took her back out front to show her how to ring someone up. It was easy enough, though the system was a little outdated. Daisy walked her through the process with a few customers who were coming through. Charlotte even suggested another book by a similar author to a customer, who ended up buying even more books than she came in to get. Charlotte totally understood—it was impossible to leave with just one book, as hard as she tried.

By the midmorning, Charlotte had a good feel for what to do, so Daisy left her to man the cash register. Charlotte let out a slow breath, feeling the jitters fade away. She could handle this. It was already going well.

"Hey, welcome!" Charlotte said when Elise walked through the door. Seeing a familiar face only brightened her day more.

"Hey! Is it your first day?" Elise propped her sunglasses on top of her head, revealing her smiling eyes.

"Yep!" Charlotte said with a warm smile. "Can I help you with anything?"

"I ordered a book that's just been delivered," Elise said. "I came to pick it up."

"Okay, cool. Just a second." Charlotte turned and scanned the small shelf under the desk that held customer orders. She easily found Elise's book. "Here it is. And it looks like you pre-paid?"

"Perfect." Elise took the book and smiled. "And yep, I already paid. This book has been out for a little while, but I still see it recommended all over the place."

"I've heard good things about it," Charlotte said. It was a business and personal development book, which usually wasn't Charlotte's go-to genre, but it seemed to offer much more grounded advice than other books on the same topic.

"Oh, hi, Elise!" Daisy said, sweeping into the floor of the shop from the back office. "You got your book?"

"Yep, Charlotte helped me!" Elise held up the book a little bit.

"I'm glad she did. It's been wonderful so far," Daisy gushed. "Just having an extra set of hands is great—I've gotten more done this morning than I have in ages by myself. And Charlotte's knowledge of the publishing industry has been so invaluable already."

Charlotte's cheeks flushed a little, though she was also happy to hear Daisy's compliments. It was nice to know that her experience at a publishing house wasn't going to waste. In some ways, the store was a blank slate. She already had some ideas to run by Daisy for programs and events to bring in more customers. It didn't have a website or social media profile at all, not even a Facebook page, so Charlotte could really create a brand and a following.

The store was already so popular without having much of a presence online that having one would only boost sales, especially in younger demographics.

All of the possibilities excited her, and it was only her first day.

"That's amazing!" Elise grinned, hugging her book to her chest and turning to Charlotte. "I've been trying to help my dad at his restaurant, but that help involves asking him to hire someone else to help. I swear, sometimes I think he just wants to be tired."

"I understand where he's coming from. Sometimes it's hard to give a little piece of your business to someone else, especially when you've built it from the ground up." Daisy sighed. "But it's well worth it."

"I should get you to come talk to my dad," Elise said with a laugh. "That's a great pitch if I've ever heard one."

Daisy laughed too. "Oh, he's so stubborn. There's no way he'll listen."

* * *

Elise tucked her receipt into the book she'd bought for her dad, stepping out onto the street again. Seeing how thrilled Daisy was with Charlotte's help after less than a day really boosted her mood. Hiring some help for her father had the potential to make a massive difference. He wouldn't have to wake up at five in the morning every single day and not stop until late at night.

And she hoped the book would help too. It was short and to the point, giving all the logical reasons why everyone needed to slow down to enjoy life more. Her father was excellent at fighting logical arguments with excuses, but a lot of the reviews had said that the book knew just how to refute those common arguments.

Sliding on her sunglasses again, she looked down the block and spotted the familiar head of dark blonde hair of her best friend, looking down at his phone with a cup of iced coffee in hand.

"Gabe!" Elise called. He looked up and smiled, waving.

"Hey, what's up?" Gabe asked once they met in the middle of the block.

"Not much." Elise stepped out of the flow of foot traffic. "Just running some errands. I dropped by the bank, then the bookstore."

"What'd you get from the bookstore?" He tilted his head, trying to read the title while the book was under her arm. Elise helped him by holding it in front of them both. "*The New Work-Life Balance?* For your dad, I'm guessing?"

Elise grinned. "Maybe."

They started walking in the direction Elise had been going before, falling easily into step as they always did. She had known Gabe for so long that brief pauses in conversation weren't awkward in the slightest.

"Daisy just hired some help at the bookstore and she can't stop raving about her—her name is Charlotte, by the way. It's been less than a day and Daisy already feels better than she has in ages," Elise said.

"That's good news for your case trying to convince your dad to get help." Gabe gently nudged Elise with his shoulder.

"Definitely!" Elise glanced up at him, a little smile in her eyes. "Also, I think Charlotte is single. In case you were curious. She loves books, of course, and she's really nice. Plus, she's pretty."

Gabe just rolled his eyes, which Elise had come to expect from him on this topic.

"Come on, Gabe," Elise continued. "You should give someone new a shot. You haven't even dated anyone in over a year."

His divorce had been finalized for a little longer than that. She understood his reluctance—it probably wasn't easy to enter the dating scene in your mid-thirties in a somewhat small town. But she knew Gabe well too. He was a great guy and deserved to have someone special in his life, especially after such a rough patch.

"There's no one I'm really interested in," he said quietly, shrugging and looking at a point far off in the distance.

Elise shrugged too. "I'm just saying."

"I know, Elise. I know."

She didn't want to push him, so she decided to shift gears.

"Anyway, what are you up to in town besides getting coffee?" Elise asked.

"Same as you—boring errands." Gabe raised his coffee cup. "But at least there's coffee at the end of it."

"And some sunshine." Elise smiled, stopping at a corner. "Which way are you heading?"

"To the left. You?"

"To the right." Elise gave him a quick hug. "It was nice bumping into you."

"Yeah, nice bumping into you too." Gabe patted her shoulder and started walking. "Good luck with your dad."

"Thanks!"

She knew she'd need all the luck she could get.

CHAPTER TWELVE

Charlotte twisted the cap off a bottle of red wine and poured herself a glass to enjoy while she finished cooking dinner. It wasn't fancy in the slightest, but she didn't mind. She felt a lot less stressed about her finances now that she had been at her bookstore job for two weeks, but she wouldn't have splurged on expensive wine even if she were being paid a lot more.

She set a timer for the vegetables she had roasting and pulled out a pan to start cooking some chicken thighs. Her phone rang from its spot on the window looking out onto the backyard—it was Nina.

"Hey!" Charlotte said, cradling her phone between her elbow and her ear. "Just a second, let me get my earbuds so I can use my hands."

She dug around in the chaos of the living room and found them, connecting them to her phone and tucking her phone into her pocket.

"Are you cooking dinner?" Nina asked.

"Yep, just some chicken thighs and a bunch of roasted veggies. I've got some couscous too. Is having both couscous and potatoes overkill?" Charlotte went over to her fridge to grab the chicken.

"No, do whatever you want. It's not like you're eating Trix and candy bars for dinner."

"True. Thanks for validating my carb choices." Charlotte smiled. "I might get a little fancy and make a sauce, but I'm not sure yet."

"Sounds like you're all settled in," Nina said. "How's work going?"

"Really good! It's been so nice actually selling the books to people and talking about them." Charlotte adjusted the heat on the stove. "And Daisy is great too."

"I'm glad to hear it." Charlotte could hear the smile in Nina's voice. "Oh, and how's Bruno?"

"He's really good." Charlotte looked over to Bruno's favorite spot, sitting on his bed with a view outside. "He likes to watch me cook."

"Probably to swoop in and get anything that you drop."

"Yup." Charlotte laughed. "He likes fruit the most for some reason. I was eating an apple on the couch the other day and he just kept looking between me and the apple from across the room the entire time. His little head kept tilting from side to side whenever I took a bite."

"Oh no, can he still not get up?"

"He can! He's a lot more mobile than he used to be, though he's limping around in his cast, but he still just stares at me across the room." Charlotte put some chicken on the pan, skin side down. "I guess I should be pleased with that since he's not in my face while I'm trying to eat, but it's just as unnerving as it is adorable."

Bruno sighed, resting his head on the ground. The sigh made him sound like he had been working all day in the office instead of lounging around. Charlotte had to smile.

"That does sound kind of adorable. You should totally keep him," Nina said. "Assuming his owner hasn't found him yet."

"No, no luck yet. I sent a picture to Miles from the animal shelter and he hasn't had any luck." Charlotte sighed and looked out the window as she washed her hands. "It might have been years since he ran away or was dumped on the side of the road, so who knows if anyone will ever claim him?"

Briggs was out back, clearing some overgrown weeds and junk that Charlotte doubted she'd keep, even if everything were in working condition. Rain had rusted some metal objects and sand had blown into any crevices in the electronics, rendering them useless. The setting sun was shining down on him, making the red of his t-shirt look even brighter.

He moved like someone who knew what he was doing, and was good at it. It was hard to not notice how attractive he was, as much as Charlotte wished she didn't. Even though the sting of being cheated on had faded a little bit, she wasn't sure if developing a crush on her handyman was a good idea for her at that point.

"You there?" Nina asked.

"Hm?" Charlotte realized that she was still absently washing her hands. They were pink from the hot water and all the scrubbing. "Yeah, I'm here."

"Were you distracted by something?"

"Eh, not really." Charlotte didn't want to get into discussing Briggs, at least not yet. She dried her hands. "So what have you been up to?"

Nina caught her sister up on her life as Charlotte finished cooking dinner. Her freelance job at the marketing firm had ended recently, so she had just begun a new marketing gig, and she was still taking a break from dating after being burned in her last relationship. Although Charlotte kept her thoughts to herself, she was surprised that Nina's "dating ban" had lasted this long. Nina was a serial dater, falling hard and fast, then getting hurt every time. Charlotte hated seeing her sister hurt, so she was glad that Nina had kept her promise to herself for so long.

Eventually Charlotte said goodbye and settled down to eat. The food was simple, but delicious—the vegetables had caramelized in the oven a bit, and the potatoes had a bit of crisp. The chicken thighs were juicy, and the quick mustard sauce she had thrown together had turned out really well, soaking into the fluffy couscous. She glanced out at Briggs again.

He had been working hard most of the day and was probably hungry. Even though she wanted to invite him in to eat with her, she didn't want to make things weird. They had talked to each other, of course, but mostly about the dog or about the work on the house. She didn't want him to feel obligated—he was just working in exchange for board.

She paused, and decided on a compromise—she could bring the food to him. After plating up another dish, she headed outside. He noticed her almost right away.

"Do you want some?" She asked, raising a dish.

He paused, then grinned. "I never turn down food that smells that good."

Charlotte headed over to a small patio table that she had saved from Jean's things, and they both settled in.

"This is delicious, thank you," he said after they had eaten for a little while.

"Sure, no problem," Charlotte said with a shrug. "I figured that you'd be hungry from working all day and I always make extra."

"My appetite's pretty big whether I'm working or not." He chuckled.

"So is mine, but I'm not lifting a bunch of stuff all day." Charlotte laughed too. "Actually, that's not true. I've been lifting a lot of boxes of books lately."

"Moving a few boxes of hardcovers will definitely work up an appetite."

"For sure." She took a few moments to take another bite. "I can't believe there's this much stuff back here. I had no idea what I was getting into when I inherited this house. I mean, I knew my Aunt Jean liked a lot of different things, but not *this* many things. Her house didn't used to look like this."

"What was it like whenever you were here before?" he asked.

"It was still a little cluttered like it is now, but there weren't many things in disrepair." Charlotte poked at a brussels sprout. "Maybe it just has to do with getting older, or maybe I didn't notice as a kid. The house still has the same feeling, though, with all these high ceilings."

"So it's like realizing that something you thought was enormous as a kid was actually not that big?"

"I guess so." Charlotte paused, gathering her thoughts. "I used to come here almost every summer, but then we abruptly stopped when I was a teenager."

"What happened?"

"I think there was a falling out between my aunt and my mom, but I'm not totally sure," Charlotte said. "And my mom's not the type of person to be open about things like that. She's very put-together and likes order."

"Like the dog thing you mentioned at the vet's office."

"Just like that. Everything in her home is spotless and I doubt she'd ever let it get even a tenth as messy as Jean's house." Charlotte looked off at the beach. "But that was kind of what made visiting fun. Jean was always up for any adventure and loved doing all the messy things that my mom didn't. She never married and had this carefree energy that I loved."

"You must miss her."

"I do." Charlotte swallowed. "I wish I'd had more time with her than I did. But now this place feels like it's filled with weird memories. Good ones, yeah, but then I think about the possible reasons why we never came back after a while."

Briggs nodded, seeming to understand. Charlotte was surprised at how easy it was to open up to him about this. Maybe it was the way he listened, like he was taking everything in and really processing it.

"Hm. Then what made you come back?" he asked after chewing for a few moments.

"I just needed a fresh start." She sighed, though the burn of one of the worst days in her life had faded slightly. "I got dumped and fired in the same day. Then I found out that Jean had passed suddenly too, so it felt like a sign. "

"Wow, that's rough."

"Yeah, it was definitely a top tier bad day." Charlotte laughed, sipping her wine. "At least with my job it was financial—the company had a bad quarter. With my ex, I saw him on a date with another woman right near my office.

"That's even worse." He winced. "Whoever dumped and cheated on you is an idiot."

Charlotte had to smile at that, though she didn't know how else to respond. She especially didn't know what to think about the gentleness in his eyes, or the empathy. It made her like him even more. There hadn't been an ounce of judgment as she explained her messy past. She had the feeling that he had his own tumultuous path too.

"What about you?" Charlotte asked, her cheeks flushed from opening up the way she had. "What brought you to Sea Breeze Cove?"

Right away, Briggs seemed to put a little barrier up, his confident posture slumping ever so slightly. His eyes usually had a little smile in them, but they dimmed. Charlotte felt her face heat up again. She hadn't intended to make him feel uncomfortable.

"I move around a bit and this felt like a beautiful place to be." He nodded toward the ocean, which they had an excellent view of. "I guess I just like a new adventure from time to time."

Charlotte nodded, even though she could sense that there was more to his reasoning besides adventure, and she wanted to find out what else was behind his nomadic lifestyle. The more she thought about it, the more she realized that it wasn't just his motivation that interested her; she wanted to get to know Briggs better as a person too.

* * *

"Ready to go for a ride, buddy?" Briggs asked Bruno, who furiously wagged his tail in response. "Let's go."

Briggs picked Bruno up and put him into the backseat of Charlotte's car. Today he had another appointment with Dr. Gilbert. Even though Bruno wasn't Charlotte's or his, he found himself invested in the dog's care.

Both of them made sure Bruno didn't get his cast wet or dirty in his walks on the beach or baths, and they alternated who fed him. They hadn't consciously decided to work together—it just happened. He and Charlotte had made a good team.

Briggs made sure Bruno was comfortable, then got into the passenger seat as Charlotte got in on driver's side. She looked at Bruno, giving him a scratch under his chin, before pulling away.

They rode in companionable silence for the most part, only chuckling when Bruno's tail thumped against the seat when he saw a flock of birds.

"He's going to be so excited to have his cast off eventually," Charlotte said, glancing at Bruno in the rearview mirror. Briggs looked back there too. Bruno's nose was propped up against the ledge of the window, fogging up the glass. "He'll be able to chase all the birds he wants."

"I get the feeling he'll be overwhelmed. Have you seen those flocks of seagulls? It feels like there are hundreds of them."

"Oh yeah, it's going to blow his mind." Charlotte laughed, as did Briggs.

Briggs liked Charlotte a lot—she was easy to be around, and surprisingly easy to talk to. Almost dangerously easy. The other night, he had almost told her the entire story of the deaths of his wife and son, but he couldn't quite bring himself to do it.

Now he was torn—he sort of wanted to tell her, but he wasn't sure how to put it all into words. His grief and sadness and shock were so heavy in his mind, even after all these years. In some ways, he felt like it would have been easier to let Charlotte somehow see the stream of memories in his head, like a movie.

He wanted her to see the way he used to be, happy and open with people, running his own construction business. The contrast was impossible to miss, and if it were possible, it would change how she saw him, like it would ruin the easy companionship they'd quickly built.

He hated the looks of pity he got whenever he talked about their deaths. As much as he appreciated where people's sympathies came from, it only made Briggs want to shy away from them.

When they arrived at the vet's office, Briggs helped the dog out without jostling his bad leg. The excited tail wags and soft panting stopped when Bruno realized where he was. Briggs clipped his leash onto his collar, but Bruno stayed put, looking up at Briggs with big, sad eyes. The look could have melted anyone's resolve, but they couldn't hop back into the car and leave.

"I know, bud. It's not your favorite place, but we have to get that leg checked out," Briggs said gently, stretching the leash as far as he could go without pulling the dog. Reluctantly, Bruno followed, his head down. "Good boy."

"Hello! Is Mr. Bruno here for his appointment?" Pearl, the veterinary receptionist, gave a friendly smile when she spotted Bruno. Bruno's tail tentatively started wagging. He wasn't a fan of being poked and prodded, but whenever he was off the exam table, he loved everyone who worked at the clinic. Pearl was usually the one working the front desk, and she had come to adore Bruno almost as much as Briggs and Charlotte had.

"He is!" Charlotte said.

"Alright then, he'll be with you in Room Two shortly." Pearl gave Bruno a few more pats before letting them head into the room.

Bruno sat, his ears drooping a little bit, so Briggs patted his head a few times.

"Hey there," Dr. Gilbert—or Ethan, as he told them to call him—greeted as he came inside. "Hey, Bruno. Let me come down to you."

Ethan asked for Briggs to bring the dog toward the middle of the room, which he did. He then kneeled, giving Bruno a few soothing strokes before taking a look at his leg for a little bit. Bruno seemed to calm down right away, pressing his forehead against Ethan's side.

"Long story short, things are looking really good," Ethan said, looking up at them with a smile. "The cast looks good and clean, too."

"That feels like a miracle." Charlotte chuckled. "He's gotten much better at walking with the cast on and it seems like he wants to go everywhere there's dirt or sand."

"Yeah, it's a little hard to keep dogs from exploring." Ethan ran his hands along Bruno's sides.

"And it looks like he's put on a tiny bit more weight. We'll get the exact number in a bit."

"Oh, good!" Charlotte said. "I was a little worried—you mentioned he was a little underweight. He loves to eat."

"Like most dogs do," Briggs added with a chuckle.

"Oh, definitely." Ethan moved around to Bruno's front and started looking at his teeth. "As long as he's eating the dog food I recommended, it's all good."

"For the most part he does." Briggs looked to Charlotte, suppressing a smile.

He had caught her sneaking Bruno little treats here and there, and whenever she cooked, Bruno loved to wait nearby, ready to eat anything that dropped to the floor. But Briggs knew he wasn't blameless either. He'd snuck Bruno little pieces of ham from time to time too. The dog had gotten a taste for it after that first night when Charlotte found him.

"Yeah, he gets a little bit of human food. He really loves fruit." Charlotte looked a little embarrassed. "Well, only apple slices and blueberries, but those are a once in a while treat."

"And ham," Briggs added.

"That's fine as long as he's digesting everything

well and it's not a daily thing." Ethan smiled up at her. "He looks really good overall—it's obvious that he's being well cared for. Bruno is lucky you found him."

Charlotte smiled back at him.

Ethan quickly wrapped up the rest of his exam, giving Bruno a clean bill of health. Bruno seemed extremely happy to walk out of the examination room, earning a treat from Pearl. Briggs came down to the dog's level and gave him extra pets for being good, making the dog's tail go wild.

"Okay, so we'll need to see Bruno again in a few weeks," Ethan said, stepping behind the reception desk across from Charlotte. "Before then, would you like to have dinner with me?"

"Oh, dinner?" Charlotte's eyes widened a little bit, the tips of her ears flushing red. She glanced down at Briggs for a moment, then shrugged. "Sure, okay. I'd like that."

Briggs focused on petting Bruno, just because it would keep him calm. Something inside his gut churned. He wasn't sure why, but he didn't like Charlotte's answer.

CHAPTER THIRTEEN

Charlotte walked into the bookstore and headed to the room where they held book club. Since the book club was held in the evening, she'd had a couple hours after work to run home and grab dinner before returning to the store.

She knew the shop in and out now and took a few glances at the new arrivals and other books that she'd shelved just days before. Some of them were selling fast, including one of her personal favorites that she'd given prominent placement in the "books our staff loves" section. It was a book that hadn't blown up any bestseller lists, but she adored it anyway.

Few things were as satisfying as having a regular customer who seemed on the fence about the book come in and rave to her about how much they loved it.

"Hey, guys!" Charlotte said, waving to Sadie, Addison, and Elise, who saved her a seat. "What's up?"

"Not much!" Elise said, turning toward Charlotte. "I've *finally* gotten somewhere with my dad. He's thinking about shifting some things around in his business and hiring some more help. I think the book helped."

"That's great news!"

Charlotte had heard a lot more of Elise's stories about her father's devotion to the restaurant and just how much he resisted slowing down. She could see why he worked so much, though. Firefly Bistro was always busy whenever she walked by and she still thought about the delicious pasta she'd had when Elise invited her and the girls to dinner there once. It had been such a simple dish—a red meat sauce—but the flavors melted on her tongue and turned into something spectacular.

"I'm so relieved." Elise laughed. "I was running out of possible options to convince him. Next it was going to be a full-on intervention."

"I would have come," Addison said. "He deserves to rest."

"Thank you," Elise said. "He's always like, 'it's a well-oiled machine back here, Elise!' and I keep on telling him that every machine needs a tune up."

"That's true," Sadie said. "I've been working on my business plan and I keep wishing I could come close to something that looks like a machine. I know I won't be a perfect business owner straight out of the gate but there's so much to it! Those business classes in college didn't prepare me for this."

"Oh, for your doggy daycare?" Addison asked. Sadie nodded. "You'll definitely figure it out! It's exciting that you're making the leap."

"I'm super nervous, but I think it's time to stop thinking about it and start doing it." Sadie's cheeks flushed and she looked at the book in her lap. "Anyway, enough about me. How are you, Charlotte? How are things with Bruno?"

"Bruno's great! He got a clean bill of health when we went to the vet, and he's gained a little bit of weight." Charlotte smiled. "He's moving around much more too. Here, I took a little video of him watching some birds that flew into the backyard."

Charlotte dug out her phone and pulled up the video, holding it so everyone could see. The video showed Bruno standing at one of the floor to ceiling windows, his nose in the air and tail wagging furiously as he tried to look at every bird at the same time. Everyone laughed, and they watched the short clip again before Charlotte put her phone away.

"He's so sweet," Sadie said with a gentle sigh. "That little face of his makes him look so happy all the time."

"Yeah, it's great to come home and have him happy to see me," Charlotte said, pausing. "Oh, and also, I have a date soon."

"Really? With who?" Addison leaned forward, her eyes bright with curiosity.

"With Ethan. He asked me out after Bruno's last appointment." Charlotte's cheeks warmed up thinking back to the moment he had asked her. She hadn't intended to look at Briggs before answering, but she had and she couldn't figure out why. He hadn't seemed too put off by it, and it wasn't like they were together anyway.

"That's so exciting! He's a really nice guy," Sadie said. "Pretty much all of my clients go to him and always have great things to say."

"He really is nice. Bruno still hates going to the vet, but once Ethan's done poking at him, he adores him." Charlotte chuckled.

"Okay guys, let's get this book club started," Daisy said, coming into the room with a flourish, her long sun dress flowing behind her. "I loved this one and I hope you all did too."

Everyone settled in as Daisy started up the discussion of their latest book, a family saga that spanned several generations and countries. It wasn't something that Charlotte would have usually picked up, but she enjoyed it anyway. Working at the store and talking about books with all kinds of people had really opened up Charlotte's reading tastes more than ever before.

Happiness flitted through Charlotte's chest as Daisy turned the floor over to everyone else. A few people jumped in right away, one who loved the book and the other who had issues with it. They launched into a warm debate that made Charlotte smile. She never had anything like this back in Chicago—a place that felt just right. She loved it. It was finally starting to feel like home.

Addison quietly shut the front door so she wouldn't wake her daughter, then headed into the living room where her husband Jesse was watching TV on low volume. He turned and smiled as Addison pressed a kiss to his forehead, letting her lips linger there for a moment. His scent was comforting, a bit like the soap he used to get grease off his hands at his auto repair shop and something that she couldn't quite pinpoint.

"Lainey's sleeping?" Addison asked.

"Yep, or at least she should be."

"Did she not want to go to bed?"

"Not really, even though we played outside for a long time. But I read her a few books until she finally conked out," he said. "And by a few, I mean the same three in rotation."

"As always." Addison shook her head and smiled. "I bought a few new ones at the bookstore that I hope she'll like. Let me go kiss her good night."

Addison ruffled his shaggy brown hair as she walked past him, down the hall toward Lainey's room. Her penguin-shaped nightlight was on, gently illuminating her face. Animals were Lainey's favorite at the moment, so they decorated the room with a horse bedspread and cute animal drawings Addison had stumbled upon at a craft fair.

Opening the door a little wider, Addison slipped inside and kissed Lainey on the forehead, her heart filling with warmth as it always did at the sight of her daughter sleeping so peacefully. She left just as quietly as she came and went back to Jesse, curling up on the couch next to him.

"How was book club?" He asked, gently playing with the hair at the nape of her neck.

"Really good! Lots of great conversation and laughs. Loved the book too," Addison said, leaning into his touch.

"I thought it had made you mad?"

"Oh, it did, but because I wanted to shake some sense into the characters. It all worked out in the end." Addison pulled her knees up onto the couch. "And all the girls are doing well too. Charlotte has a date with Ethan, the vet at the little clinic. And Elise is making headway on getting her dad to hire help."

"Finally, it feels like he's been reluctant forever." Jesse laughed.

"I know! I almost can't believe it, but she's been wearing him down little by little. I guess being successful in business, especially in the restaurant world, takes a little stubbornness, but even stubbornness runs out eventually."

"You know from experience, huh?" Jesse nudged her and she laughed. He had run the local auto body shop for a while now and had everything under control, but things were a little more chaotic at the beginning. He'd said he had it all handled, but Addison could see where he was refusing to ask for help.

"You're different." She kissed his forehead. "And speaking of entrepreneurs, Sadie's finally putting together her business plan for her doggy daycare."

"Yeah? Then we'll have a place for that puppy Lainey has been begging for." Jesse gave her a knowing smile.

"Oh goodness, no." Addison snorted. Just the thought of her rambunctious five year-old plus an equally energetic puppy made her tired. Almost instantly, the humor left her.

"What's up?" Jesse asked, his voice gentle.

"I was just thinking that I'd like to give Lainey a sibling instead." Addison sighed and Jesse gently massaged the back of her neck.

They had wanted another child for a while, but it wasn't working out. Some days it hit Addison hard, especially when she saw her friends having more children. It was always strange to be simultaneously happy for someone, sad, and a little jealous. She loved Lainey dearly and was grateful to have her, but she had always imagined having a family of at least four.

"Hey, listen." Jesse's brown eyes were reassuring. "It's all going to work out like it's meant to, okay? Let's just take things one day at a time."

Addison smiled, sliding closer to her husband

and tucking herself under his arm before placing a kiss on the side of his jaw. Even though they had been together for years, she still marveled at how easily he was able to calm her down with a few words.

She really hoped he was right.

CHAPTER FOURTEEN

Charlotte smoothed her hands over her dark blue sundress and looked at herself in her big, heavy bedroom mirror. The mirror had been tucked behind an armoire in Jean's bedroom even though it was in beautiful shape, with an ornate frame and without a single scratch on it. It had to have been expensive.

Charlotte stepped a little closer. She had put her auburn hair into a bun and put on a little more makeup than usual. With all the sun she was getting, she hadn't needed to put on much blush or bronzer to look fresh. All in all, she felt good about how she looked.

Tonight was her date with Ethan. It had been a long time since she had been on a first date, and she wasn't sure if Ethan was going to notice. She took a deep breath and let it out. It was going to be fine—she had liked talking to him when she had visited his office for Bruno's appointments and he was friendly. This was just more of that.

The doorbell rang downstairs and Charlotte rushed down, grabbing her purse and opening the door.

"Hey," Ethan said when she opened the door. "You look beautiful."

"Thank you." Charlotte put her purse on her shoulder, her cheeks flushing as she noticed the small bouquet he was holding. "You look nice too."

He was wearing a green button-down shirt that was the same color as his eyes, and dark pants. His sandy brown hair was a little tidier than it was when she saw him last, like he'd gotten it cut.

"These are for you, by the way." He handed her the bouquet.

"They're beautiful, thank you." Charlotte brought them to her nose and took a sniff. "Let me put them in a vase really quick."

She went back inside and easily found a vase, filling it with water and putting the flowers on the kitchen counter. Ethan waited patiently outside and smiled at her again when she returned.

The drive to the restaurant was pleasant and

short, filled with small talk and pointing out the views. He knew a lot of spots that Charlotte hadn't heard of or noticed before, places she made a mental note to return to.

Ethan had picked out a place he had heard great things about down near the water—a nice little seafood place. The outside looked like it had been renovated recently in contrast to the buildings nearby, but it didn't look entirely out of place. They were greeted right away by a friendly host, who found a waiter to take them to the table Ethan had reserved.

"I highly recommend the catch of the day, which comes with a fresh orzo salad," the waiter said as he sat them down. "Enjoy."

Charlotte looked over the menu. "Wow, this all looks so good."

"Yeah, it does." Ethan's eyes were bright with excitement. "What's catching your eye?"

"Hm, definitely some seafood..." Charlotte paused, then both of them laughed. "That doesn't narrow anything down at all, does it?"

"Nope. But are you thinking more shellfish, or fish-fish? My friend said the crab was incredible." Ethan glanced up at the sign that displayed the catch of the day and what fishery had caught it.

"I think I'll go with the catch of the day," Charlotte said, closing her menu. "It's catching my eye, if you'll excuse that horrendous pun. It sounds good.""

"That was pretty groan-worthy, but I'll excuse it." Ethan smiled. "I'll get the crab, then."

The waiter came by and took their orders, suggesting a bottle of wine that would accompany both dishes well. He quickly returned with it, pouring them each a glass with a flourish. Charlotte and Ethan clinked their glasses and took a sip.

It was a white; a really nice one, from what Charlotte could tell. Definitely better than the kind she bought regularly. It was cool and crisp, and felt like it would be a great drink to have while sitting on the beach.

"So you heard about this restaurant from a friend?" Charlotte asked.

"Yeah, a friend of mine from childhood. We grew up down the street from each other," Ethan said. "I'm pretty sure his parents still live in that house. I know my parents are still there."

"Wow, so you were born and raised here?" Charlotte swirled her wine in the glass, though she wasn't sure what that was supposed to do for the wine's flavor. "That's how you knew all those cool spots on our drive?"

"Yeah, I was." Ethan's smile was tinged with pride. "I only went away for college, then vet school. It just feels like home here, in a way that nowhere else has."

"It's so lovely here; I understand that. I'm already getting settled in," Charlotte said. "Did you always plan on coming back?"

"Hm..." Ethan looked at a spot past her head, out of one of the many windows along the side of the restaurant. The sunlight hit his eyes in a way that made them look as vividly green as fresh grass. They were beautiful, but Charlotte didn't feel her heart speed up when she noticed them. "Kind of. I'm pretty close to my family, so I knew I would have at least stayed in-state. But then there was an opportunity to work at the clinic under the vet who used to run it, so I took it. I guess that might make me seem a little boring, eh?"

"No, not at all. I understand the appeal. And there's nothing wrong with wanting to stick close to family."

Ethan's smile broadened at that. "Yeah. I was one of those kids who always wanted to be a vet, so I guess I always imagined a life kind of like this. Going to the beach, walks on the boardwalk, picnics..."

"Helping dogs," Charlotte added.

"Definitely. And their owners." His smile turned boyish for a moment before he got serious. "Having a sick or injured dog weighs on you."

"I know. Bruno's not even mine and I was so worried about him that night. I tossed and turned like crazy." Charlotte's heart softened, thinking about what a sorry state Bruno was in before. "But now he's doing so well, thanks to you."

Ethan looked down, chuckling. "I'm glad I could help him. He's a good dog."

"He is. I wonder where he came from." Charlotte sipped her wine. "He seems like he's been socialized around people, but he also looked like he hadn't had a good meal in a while."

"People dump dogs more often than I like to think about. Maybe he got by from being fed by strangers. I've seen that happen a lot of times, especially when people want to help but can't bring a dog into their home because they have cats or allergies or something." A little tension came into his eyes. "Sorry, I get a little mad at the idea of people abandoning dogs."

"It's okay. I get upset too." Charlotte tried to think about a better topic. "Do you have any funny dog stories?"

"I have way too many." Ethan's face brightened again. "Just the other day, I had an owner come in with a chocolate lab who I've been seeing since he was a puppy. Labs are a little notorious for their appetites and this dog—Norman—isn't any different."

"Norman is a slightly ridiculous name for a dog."

"Oh, that's not even the weirdest one I've come across." Ethan's smile broadened. "But anyway, I was talking to the owner about their new baby and how Norman was adjusting. They said everything was fine with Norman, but she was worried about the baby losing socks."

Charlotte pressed her lips together, holding back a smile. She could sense where this was going.

"When I took an x-ray of him since he seemed to be having digestive upset, and there were six baby socks in his stomach."

"Oh no," Charlotte said with a laugh. "I'm guessing he was okay?"

"He was—it was just a waiting game and it wasn't the first time he'd ever gotten into something he shouldn't have. He's very lucky."

The conversation drifted to more ups and down of being a small town vet, and stories about growing up in Sea Breeze Cove. The food was delicious, too—Charlotte's snapper was perfectly fresh and flaky, and the orzo salad was just light enough for a summer evening. The bite of Ethan's crab dish that she had was almost so good that she almost wished she had ordered it instead.

"Want to take a walk?" Ethan asked after picking up the bill.

"Sure, that sounds lovely." It was a beautiful evening, as it often was here.

They walked outside, falling into step next to each other on the boardwalk. It was lively and filled with people who were also walking off meals or enjoying the early evening.

"Oh look, there's an ice cream place," Charlotte said. "Mind if I pick up the tab for something?"

"Sure, I don't mind that. Do you want to split something?" Ethan stopped in front of the small ice cream stand.

"How about a sundae?"

"Sure!"

They ordered a peanut fudge sundae and stood at one of the standing tables in front of the stand. It was a great spot to people watch, and a beautiful evening overall, but for some reason, Charlotte felt like she was just having a nice time instead of an incredible one. The conversation was good, as was the food, and she didn't sense any first date awkwardness from either of them. Ethan had been nothing but a gentleman.

She and Ethan finished the sundae, chatting about the dinner they'd just had and the things they were looking forward to doing in the upcoming week, then walked back to his car. The more she thought about it, the more it made sense—she liked Ethan, but there just weren't any sparks there. And after everything that had happened with Peter, she wasn't sure if she wanted to jump into something else with both feet.

He drove her home and walked her to her door.

"I had a nice time tonight," Charlotte said, her heart rate picking up for all the wrong reasons. Was he going to kiss her? She wasn't sure if she wanted the date to end on that note.

"I did too." Ethan smiled, then kissed her on the cheek, to Charlotte's relief. "See you later."

* * *

Briggs was stretched out in bed reading an old paperback Charlotte had loaned him when he heard a car pull up, then away a few moments later. It wasn't super late. For some reason, he was glad that it wasn't. Maybe that meant Charlotte's date was just okay.

He ran a hand through his hair and yawned. Then again, whether her date was good or not didn't matter. He wasn't going to be there long, so it didn't matter who Charlotte dated. If he were her friend, he'd hope that she found someone great. He'd be happy for her since she was an amazing woman who deserved a man who wouldn't cheat on her the way she had been cheated on before.

But still. He was glad she was home.

He tucked his bookmark into his book, kissed his fingers, then pressed them to the photo of his wife and son. As he slid under the covers and started to drift off, he could almost hear his wife's voice in his head, calling him a stubborn fool with a playful laugh.

* * *

Charlotte huffed and got out of bed, having tossed and turned for a little while. She looked around the master bedroom for something to help her drift off to sleep. The book she was reading was too good and exciting to let her fall asleep easily, so something else had to do.

Jean had loved books just as much as Charlotte did, so there were plenty of options. Unfortunately, Charlotte had sifted through most of the options in the bedroom and felt like those options would keep her up. Maybe there was something she had missed.

After some digging, she found a little leather-bound book in a drawer. It had to be Jean's. She flipped it open, revealing handwritten pages—an old diary. That definitely piqued her curiosity. She wandered back to the bed and sat down on the edge, looking through the first few pages.

She had never opened the letters addressed to her mom, but she couldn't help herself from opening the diary and reading a few pages, sliding under the covers again. The first pages she fell on were early entries, and from the date on the pages, Charlotte knew she had to have been around twelve and Nina was around seven.

I'm so excited for Melissa, Hugh, and the girls to finally arrive. I have a lot planned already, but these visits always end up better when we just play things by ear. There's the beach, of course, and a craft fair that should be fun. And so many new places to eat—even though Nina can be a little picky, I know she'll love these places.

Charlotte smiled, nostalgia washing over her. She remembered that summer. Nina had loved all the food that Jean exposed them to, which had turned Nina into an adventurous eater as an adult. Their mother had been completely bewildered as to how Jean got Nina to eat ceviche, when at home, trying to get her to eat anything but chicken nuggets was a struggle.

Jean always had a fun activity planned too, sometimes for all of them, sometimes for just Charlotte and Nina. If Charlotte was remembering that particular trip correctly, Jean had taken them on a hike.

The next entry was dated a little while later, written in green pen.

I suppose this is what a diary is for, but it feels a little bit cliche. But it doesn't matter—this is just for me. I have feelings for a man for the first time in ages. I'm not sure if he's even noticed me, but I can't help but notice him.

Charlotte's eyes started to droop, so she slid a

paper bookmark she'd taken from the bookstore into the diary and put it on her side table. It would be there for her in the morning, and although she was curious to know more about this aunt of hers who was so distant for most of her life, she welcomed the feeling of oncoming sleep even more.

CHAPTER FIFTEEN

Charlotte let out a sigh of relief after shelving the last copy of the newest thriller the bookstore had gotten in. Daisy's back wasn't what it used to be, so Charlotte had readily volunteered to take over shelving duties. But as it turned out, Charlotte's back wasn't too happy with her after her first few days of picking up boxes and bending over to get things on the bottom shelves.

Now after a few weeks of working there, she had gotten much more used to it. She hardly felt a thing anymore. It was a much better form of exercise than anything she could do at a gym.

Everything about working at the bookstore had fallen into place easily. Charlotte had a great lay of the land, knowing exactly where the most commonly requested books were in moments, and she was starting to recognize some of the regulars who came in.

Daisy was a dream boss, too. She loved hearing Charlotte's feedback about how to improve the store and they had already implemented a few of her ideas. They had gotten a new checkout system that made it easier for customers to pay and get receipts via email and made a website too.

In slow periods, Charlotte started to work on setting up more author events and readings to bring in more customers. The upstairs space was perfect for signings and it wasn't used nearly enough. It was ambitious, but Charlotte could see multiple events every week from book clubs to professional mixers.

Charlotte folded up the empty box and put it in the back with the others, humming quietly to herself as she walked back into the store. There were two customers, one who had said they were just browsing and the other who bought a new romance at least twice a week. Charlotte sat behind the front desk, opening up her laptop to add more to her potential author signing list, but hardly got the document up before the door flew open.

It was Addison, her blond hair in a haphazard bun on top of her head and her hazel eyes wide. She had come in with all the momentum of someone who was rushing from place to place, only to abruptly slam on the brakes—a little dazed, and very uncertain.

"Hey, Addison!" Charlotte said, closing the laptop. "Can I help you today?"

"Hey! And no thank you." Addison paused, biting her lip. Charlotte raised an eyebrow, studying her friend a little more. Addison dressed somewhat casually in t-shirts and shorts, but today, her outfit looked a little rumpled, as if she'd thrown it on. Upon closer inspection, her shirt was on backward.

"Your shirt's on —"

"Backward?" Addison cut Charlotte off, trying to look at the neckline of her shirt. "I'm a mess. I'll fix it later. Actually, since I'm clearly in need of some help, can I ask you for a favor? A non-book favor?"

"Sure, shoot."

"Would you be available to babysit Lainey on Friday night?" Addison asked. "We've been really stressed lately since we're trying for another baby. Jesse made plans for this amazing fancy dinner at home because he wanted to do something nice for me."

"That's really sweet of him."

"It is." Addison played with her necklace, a small

smile coming onto her face. "We want to enjoy each other's company and reconnect without being interrupted. Even if I put Lainey to bed she still likes to resist falling asleep until we're all too tired to stay up."

Charlotte nodded. She had been a babysitter for kids Lainey's age in college and some days she wished she could absorb their energy for herself. They clearly had extra.

"Sometimes I feel like we're always rushing around and only get a chance to talk when we're about to pass out asleep," Addison continued. "Anyway, Lainey's regular sitter and back-up sitter are both busy that night, so I've been rushing around trying to find a replacement. Are you available?"

"Sure," Charlotte said. "I'd be happy to help."

* * *

Addison's car came up the driveway as Charlotte watched from the front porch, testing the step her foot had put a hole through on her first day. It was as if the stair never had a weakness at all. Briggs had done an amazing job getting the most pressing house repairs done, not that Charlotte ever doubted him.

She just didn't want anything to happen to Lainey while she was at the house.

Lainey was like many five year olds—filled with energy—and came rushing out of the car, skipping. Addison hustled out after her, a Hello Kitty backpack in hand.

"Hey, Lainey!" Charlotte said with a grin. "Are you excited to have fun tonight?"

"Yeah!" Lainey rushed up the stairs, her pigtails bobbing.

"Thank you so, so much, Charlotte," Addison said, finally catching up. "Here's her bag—there are her favorite toys and a few coloring books she's fond of. As for food, pizza is fine since we usually have pizza on Friday nights."

"No problem!" Charlotte took the bag. "Pizza sounds perfect anyway."

"Have fun with Charlotte, okay?" Addison said, squatting down in front of Lainey.

"Okay!" Lainey said, giving her mom a hug.

"I'll text you when we're on our way to pick her up." Addison kissed Lainey on the forehead and stood up. "And let me know if you have any questions. I'll have my phone on me."

"I'll let you guys have your date—don't worry about us."

"You're such a lifesaver, thank you."

Addison hugged Charlotte tightly and left.

"My dog friend Bruno is here," Charlotte said, pausing with her hand on the doorknob. "He's a very nice boy, but —"

"A dog?" Lainey's eyes widened in excitement. "What kind?"

Charlotte smiled. For a moment she worried that Lainey would be afraid and that she would have to put Bruno behind a dog gate for the evening. Then she remembered Addison's text in their group chat, detailing the list of animal facts that Lainey bombarded her with as she was trying to put her to bed. Everyone had laughed at Addison's mixture of desperation for Lainey to go to bed and genuine confusion as to where her daughter learned so much about lemurs.

"I'm not sure! He's a lot of different kinds of dogs mixed together." Charlotte opened the door. Bruno was standing there, wagging his tail. Before Lainey could rush him, Charlotte took her hand. "Let's let him say hello first so we don't startle him."

Lainey nodded as if she had been given a serious mission, as Charlotte patted her leg. Bruno trotted up to them, sniffing Lainey curiously and making her giggle. Lainey petted his head, beaming when his tail whipped back and forth even faster.

"He likes me!" Lainey said, looking up at Charlotte.

"He really does." Charlotte scratched Bruno above his tail. "How about we order some pizza like your mom said, then we can play with your dolls outside while we wait for it?"

"Yeah!"

Charlotte ordered the pizza—half cheese, half pepperoni—and they headed out back with all of Lainey's dolls and a picnic blanket. Bruno stretched out next to the blanket, almost as if he were going to play too. The only sounds were the ocean and Briggs hammering away at something on the side of the house.

"Okay, let's see what kind of cool dolls you have." Charlotte opened up the Hello Kitty backpack. "Which ones are your favorite?"

"The one with pink hair, and this mermaid, and this ballerina, and this cat," Lainey said, pulling out all the dolls and their accessories. "They're all friends, but the mermaid has to go live in the ocean again so they're going with her."

Charlotte smiled. "Okay, which one do you want to be?"

Lainey picked up each of the dolls, then handed Charlotte a few of them. They hadn't been playing long when Charlotte realized that Lainey had vastly simplified her story—the mermaid had to battle a wizard in order to find a secret treasure deep in the ocean, and the only one who could help her was the cat figurine, who may have been able to move things with her mind. Charlotte did her best to keep up with Lainey's creative leaps until they were both overcome with laughter.

"Sorry to interrupt," Briggs said, coming up and putting his work gloves into his pocket.

"No worries. Briggs, this is Addison's daughter Lainey. Lainey, this is my friend Briggs—he's helping me fix up the house."

"Nice to meet you, Lainey," Briggs said with a smile. "I just found a few of these old coins on the other side of the house, like they were put there on purpose. I'm not sure if they're worth anything, but I figured I'd show you."

Briggs knelt down next to the dog and showed off the coins. They were unusual and definitely old.

"Wow, like secret treasure," Lainey said, looking at the coins intently.

"Yeah, just like that." Briggs' voice was gentle. "Are your dolls looking for treasure?"

"Mmhm!" Lainey picked up the small plastic treasure chest. "But they have figured out how to work together to get it."

"Ah, I see. Teamwork is always a good thing." Briggs looked over the mess they'd made of toys, doll clothes, and other ocean-themed accessories. "Are they doing a good job of working together?"

"Mmhm, except the dolphin's a little mean sometimes," Lainey said, as if she didn't want the dolphin to overhear. "He really wants all the treasure to himself but he has to share since friends share."

"I hope he learns to be a good friend." He gave Lainey the coins, then stood again. "How about you add these to your treasure chest for now?"

"Wow, thanks!" Lainey looked at the coins, passing them from hand to hand.

Charlotte had to smile. Briggs was a kind man, but for some reason, Charlotte was surprised at how easily he spoke with Lainey, like he had been around kids before and had fun. Seeing this side of him was oddly entrancing and only deepened her curiosity about his past.

A car came up the driveway with a sign that said Sunrise Pizza on top of it, breaking her out of her trance.

"Pizza!" Lainey said, perking up.

"Want to stay for dinner?" Charlotte asked Briggs, getting to her feet as well. "We've got plenty of pizza."

Briggs hesitated for a moment before saying, "Sure, pizza sounds great."

Charlotte met the pizza guy at the front porch and Briggs helped her bring the pizza in. Bruno was incredibly interested in this development, following Briggs with his nose in the air. They sat at the table and split up the pizza, Bruno sitting underneath at their feet in case someone dropped some pepperoni,.

It was late afternoon, and the sun was just starting to appear golden above the sea, streaming in through the window. The kitchen nook was one of Charlotte's favorite spots in the house for this reason, and being able to share a meal with people here was something she wanted to do more often. She made a mental note to start seriously looking into easy dinner party menus so she could have the girls over.

"Does Bruno like pizza?" Lainey asked, looking down at the dog. Bruno, sensing that he had the best shot of a stray pepperoni with her, scooted forward on his belly and looked up at her with big, sad eyes.

"I think Bruno likes everything." Charlotte laughed. "But this is people food, so we can't give him any."

"Not even a little?" Lainey looked up at Charlotte with a look that nearly melted her heart.

"He might get a tummy ache," Briggs said, folding a slice of pizza in half. "And we don't want that—he won't be able to play later."

"Oh no." Lainey looked down at her plate, almost horrified. "I want to play later. No pizza for Bruno."

Charlotte and Briggs chuckled, digging into their food.

"Can Bruno play with us and my dolls?" Lainey asked.

"Yeah, why not? What do you think he should be?" Charlotte pulled a paper napkin out of a bag and tucked it onto Lainey's lap.

"Hm..." Lainey looked down at Bruno, whose tail twitched at the possibility of her breaking Charlotte's 'no people food for dogs' rule. "He could be the one guarding the treasure. But he's really nice so he lets them have it."

"That sounds —"

"But then the dolphin is gonna be bad and try to take it," Lainey said, cutting Charlotte off with excited eyes.

"Yeah? Will Bruno help save the day?" Briggs asked.

"Mmhm."

"He seems like he'd be a great hero." Charlotte scratched his side with her toes until he rolled over onto his side, closing his eyes in contentment. "Wouldn't ya, buddy?"

As they continued to eat, Lainey brought them up to date on all of the happenings with her dolls and stuffed animals and asked more questions about the dog. When she learned that Bruno had just gotten his cast off at the vet, she started talking about her future plans to be a veterinarian *and* a marine biologist *and* a movie star.

Charlotte and Briggs couldn't hide their amusement, giving each other knowing glances as Lainey chattered excitedly. She was a sweet kid with a big imagination, which Charlotte hoped she'd hang onto as she got older.

"How about we take Bruno down to the beach to play so we can look at the sunset?" Charlotte asked as she put away the leftover pizza and Briggs put the dishes in the sink.

"Can we build sandcastles?" Lainey asked.

"Sure, why not? There should be a little bucket around here somewhere." Charlotte looked around as if it would appear out of nowhere.

"There's one out back that we can grab on the way there," Briggs said.

"Yay!" Lainey rushed toward the door.

They headed out the back door, Lainey skipping alongside Bruno.

"Let's build one here," Lainey declared, falling to her knees on the sand, right where it turned from dry sand to damp.

"Alright, then." Briggs got down on his knees with her, bucket in hand. "What do you say—want to make a castle for your mermaid?"

Charlotte stood at a slight distance as she kept an eye on Bruno while watching them make sandcastles. Briggs helped Lainey make a base for the castle, shaping wet sand into a proper shape and making Lainey laugh with a silly voice. Charlotte couldn't keep the smile off her face as she watched.

Meanwhile, Bruno tried to attack the waves, chasing after them as the water went out and running away when they came back after him. Once he gave up trying to fight the ocean, he found a huge piece of driftwood and proudly paraded it around in his mouth.

It was as if he'd never had a broken leg at all, even though his cast hadn't been off long. Ethan had asked her on another date at the appointment where he removed the cast, and she had said yes. He seemed like a good guy, and the date had been pleasant. It wouldn't hurt to see if there was something there. Maybe the lack of sparks on their first date just meant that she had to get to know him a little bit more.

Once Bruno stopped gathering driftwood, he settled down next to Lainey and Briggs, as did Charlotte. They built an amazing sandcastle, at least in Charlotte's eyes. It was much better than anything she would have made as a girl Lainey's age. It was the perfect stage to include Bruno in the role of protector of the castle and treasure, which he obediently played.

Unfortunately, he got a little bit too excited and destroyed the sandcastle, but not before Charlotte could take a picture of it to send to Addison later. Lainey didn't seem upset, though. They built another one, a slightly smaller one for Lainey's cat figurine, as the sun started to set.

"It's getting dark out—we should head inside," Charlotte said.

"Okay." Lainey pouted, but got up without fussing.

Briggs got up too, sweeping sand off his pants, and followed them back toward the house. When they reached the backyard, they stopped for a moment.

"Thanks for the pizza and the fun," Briggs said.

"Thank you, Mr. Briggs!" Lainey gave Briggs a high-five.

"Yeah, thanks for coming with us," Charlotte said.

Briggs nodded and smiled, then headed back toward the guest house. As he walked away, Charlotte couldn't help but watch. There was still so much of Briggs that remained a mystery, and she wasn't sure how she felt about that yet.

CHAPTER SIXTEEN

"I know we're close to home, buddy," Sadie said with a laugh as Franklin, a big, exuberant German Shepherd, tugged on his leash. "Once you get inside, you can gnaw on your bones and run around in your yard."

Franklin didn't seem to hear her and kept walking quickly toward his home. Once they arrived, Sadie unlocked the back gate and let him off his leash. He went sprinting in, zooming around as if he hadn't just been on a half hour walk. Sadie texted his owner a picture of him, letting her know that they were back, made sure Franklin had some water, and headed back toward town.

Walking dogs, especially ones with as much energy as Franklin, made her work up an appetite.

Luckily, there was a small bakery right on the edge of town that she liked to frequent after walking her route with Franklin. She popped in and got a donut filled with vanilla creme, biting into it as she left. It was the perfect treat after a long morning of walking—sweet, decadent, but not so heavy that she'd fall into a sugar coma.

She polished it off in almost record time and tossed the bag into a trash can. The can was in front of a store that she had never noticed before, a secondhand clothing boutique. It had a "grand opening" sign in the window between two mannequins dressed in stylish outfits that Sadie wouldn't have pegged as secondhand—they were classic, with a few trendy pieces of jewelry around the mannequin's neck.

Given the nature of dog walking, Sadie usually didn't get too dressed up during the day, but the outfits on the mannequins were so nice that she felt compelled to take a look inside. *Maybe I'll make an occasion to dress up,* she thought.

"Hello! Welcome!" a woman said from behind the counter when Sadie walked in.

"Hi!"

Sadie looked around at all the racks of beautiful clothes. There was a wall with shoes and bags on one side, which two women were perusing, and even more racks with a few customers going through them. A few more mannequins were throughout the store, each wearing inventive outfits.

"Can I help you look for anything?" the woman asked, coming up to Sadie. She was also just as stylish as the mannequins, wearing a dark blue button-up dress with a pleated skirt and heels with a strap around the ankle, topped off with geometric earrings and bright red lipstick.

"Nothing in particular—I just saw the sign and the great outfits on the mannequin and decided to look around." Sadie ran her hand over the silky sleeve of a dress. "These clothes are so beautiful!"

"Thank you! I've always been a fan of vintage and second-hand clothing, so I like to pick the best of the best," she said. "I'm Jolene Pritchard, by the way. The owner."

"Nice to meet you! I'm Sadie." They shook hands. "I walk dogs all day, so I'm definitely dressing for comfort and function most of the time. But I like to dress up from time to time."

"We have plenty of dresses!" Jolene gestured toward a rack. "And plenty of clothes that could withstand excitable dogs on the next row. You work for a dog walking business?"

"Thanks!" Sadie ran her fingers over the first dress on the rack. "And I run the business. It's still pretty small so I can run it out of my house."

Sadie felt her cheeks flush—she was proud of her work and loved what she had built, but sometimes she felt like her business couldn't compare to a big physical location like this.

"How long have you been open?" Sadie asked, shaking away her doubts about herself.

"Not too long! A little over a week."

Sadie picked up the dress that had caught her eye. "Wow, that's great! There are already so many people in here."

"I know, I'm very lucky!" Jolene looked around. "I saw the sign in the window to lease this place and just had a gut feeling that it was perfect. Great foot traffic, huge windows in the front, all of that. I called in right away and managed to get it."

Sadie thought about the sign in the window of the location she'd been eyeing for her dog daycare, worry creeping up her spine. What if she had waited too long to reach out about renting it?

"How difficult was it to start your own business? Is it hard to manage?" Sadie asked.

"It can be stressful sometimes, especially since we just opened, but it's worth the trade-off," Jolene said. "I get to be my own boss, which is amazing, and I get to make all the decisions. I'm already in love with it even though it's definitely the biggest challenge I've ever gotten myself into.

"I bet that feels really nice. The bigger the challenge, the sweeter the reward."

"It does! I never thought I could do it, but I figured I wouldn't know until I tried. Some friends gave me a little push and here I am." Jolene turned a hanger around, almost absently. "I was good at my past jobs and liked my bosses, but this is so much better."

Sadie nodded, putting the dress back down. "I'd like to start a business, so I'm always curious about people who have."

"Go for it—my only regret so far is that I waited this long to dive in!" Jolene said.

"Really?"

"Totally." Jolene smiled.

"I'm getting closer to making the jump, I think. I want to start a dog daycare near here," Sadie said.

"That sounds like a great idea! I see so many dogs around here that there's definitely a demand."

"Thank you!" Sadie looked at the dress that had caught her eye one more time. "I'll definitely come back so I can try some things on—thanks for letting me pick your brain!"

"No problem—see you soon!"

Sadie left, taking one more glance at the store over her shoulder. She felt closer to taking the leap than ever, and although a few nervous butterflies flapped in her stomach, she couldn't help the grin that spread across her face.

She was pursuing her dream, and as scary as it was, it was exhilarating too.

* * *

Charlotte blinked when she checked the time. Fifteen whole minutes had passed since she'd last picked up Jean's diary—that was slightly better than the last stretch she'd taken away from it, which had only lasted ten minutes. She had been slowly but surely cleaning the house, tidying up in areas that Briggs had finished fixing, but she kept getting distracted.

Sometimes she read the diary at night before bed, almost like a novel, and she was getting a clearer picture of Jean's life. She had really loved animals, even back then, and talked a lot about volunteering at the shelter. Charlotte had no idea that she had been as involved in it as she had been, or that she had traveled around New England as much as she had.

It was the juicier details that kept Charlotte coming back. Jean had feelings for someone, but the details were vague—all Charlotte could sense was the depth of her feelings. They were so intense. The way she described how her heart raced every time she saw him or how she felt her attention drift to him if they were in the same room sounded like something in a romance novel she had just read. Clearly whoever this man was, he had meant a lot to Jean. Charlotte wanted to find out who he was.

She sat down on a windowsill, opening the diary again. There was a short entry just detailing her daily frustrations about summer storms and a disagreement she'd had with a stranger over a pint of ice cream at the store, but on the next page, there was a long entry.

I was definitely not prepared for today even though I woke up with one of those feelings. It's almost like my body knew something was going to go wrong before it did, like how animals flee an area before a storm has even hit. Melissa and Hugh were in town, just for a quick weekend getaway without the girls, and I had all these plans.

But then, Melissa got sidelined by a headache,

leaving me and Hugh alone to grab a bite to eat. We've done it before when Melissa wanted alone time with the girls, so I didn't think much of it, besides that weird gut feeling.

Long story short, my gut was right. Hugh told me he had fallen in love with me. I honestly didn't think I'd heard him correctly, but he said it again.

Charlotte was glad she had been sitting down when she read that. Her heart started pounding out of her chest and her knees felt weak. Her father? Was this who Jean had feelings for? She had to read on.

I told him that I had feelings for someone else and that it wasn't right—he's my brother-in-law, for goodness' sake. I turned him down right away. It was so incredibly awkward. And then we had to sit there and wait for the check! And the drive home...terrible.

But now I don't know what to do. I should tell Melissa, shouldn't I? But how could I ever do that? She has absolutely no idea about this. Just the other day, she was saying how much she loved Hugh and was so happy that they were still going strong. She has the right to know, but it would hurt her so much. But I know I have to. I just need to figure out the best way to go about it. I don't think there's a way to do it that doesn't hurt.

Charlotte swallowed the tight lump in her throat. Part of her didn't want to go on, but a stronger part did. She turned the page to the next entry. There were a few spots that looked like dried tears on the paper.

I can't believe things have gone so bad so fast. I told *Hugh that I wasn't interested in him. It wasn't a situation where I said "maybe." It was a hard no, and a clear one. But Hugh told me again that he loved me while I was making coffee, and Melissa overheard.*

She came in and before I could explain, she blew up on us. She blamed us both, as if we'd been carrying on an affair for years when it was anything but that. As hard as I tried to tell her that I'd never, ever do that to her, she didn't listen. I know Melissa—she's always so composed and put-together, so seeing her yell at us like this meant that she was angrier than I'd seen her since we were teenagers.

And I made everything so much worse by waiting and trying to figure out how to tell her. I couldn't lie—I told her that this was the second time he told me this and that I turned him away, but all she got from it was that I didn't tell her immediately. Any trust between us? Gone.

I feel like my heart is literally broken. There's an ache in my chest and I can't sleep. I love Melissa. I never wanted to hurt her, but now we can't take these things back.

"Are you okay?"

Charlotte looked up with a gasp to find Briggs standing right in front of her. She hadn't even heard him come in, or noticed that she had been crying.

"N-not really." Charlotte wiped her eyes. "It's just some family stuff that I wasn't expecting."

Briggs sat down on the other side of the windowsill, putting a comforting hand on her shoulder. It was warm and settled her almost instantly. "I'm really sorry."

"Thank you." Charlotte wiped her eyes with the back of her hand. Briggs pulled a clean handkerchief from his shirt pocket and handed it to her. "And thanks for this."

"No problem." He gave her shoulder a gentle squeeze. "It comes in handy, if you'll excuse the pun."

Charlotte chuckled a little bit before her tears overwhelmed her again. Briggs didn't shy away—he just kept a steadying hand on her shoulder as she let her tears out.

CHAPTER SEVENTEEN

Charlotte was glad that her second date with Ethan was going to be more casual—a light picnic at an outdoor concert. It was a beautiful afternoon, warm and breezy, and the venue was on the beach. Ethan had asked Charlotte to bring a blanket and the wine, and he was going to bring the rest.

He had picked her up and dropped her off near the venue to find a spot for their blanket while he went to park, leaving her to wander in the crowd to search for the perfect place. There was a solid mix of people, from families to older couples, with plenty of dogs in attendance too. She wished she had thought to bring Bruno, but he had been passed out asleep in the sunlight after a long morning of playing fetch on the beach.

Once she found an empty patch of grass and laid the blanket down, she looked across the crowd of people spread out in front of the stage, trying to find Ethan. Hopefully parking hadn't been too terrible. After a little more scanning, she found him petting a big white dog and talking to the animal's owners. She had to smile.

"Ethan!" Charlotte called, waving.

Ethan looked up and nodded at her, giving the dog one more pat and saying goodbye to the dog's owners before heading over.

"Hey!" He said, jogging the last few steps up to her. "Sorry about that—ran into a dog I see."

"No problem. I bet it's a lot more pleasant to see them here than at your office, eh?" Charlotte asked. "Does this spot work for you?"

"Yeah, it works. And definitely, it's a lot nicer to see dogs out here. As painless as I try to make their visits, they just know they've gotten their shots there or a little surgery and aren't themselves." Ethan helped her lay the blanket out. "That dog was one of them—he was shaking when they brought him in, but he was happy to see me just now."

"Dogs are great like that." Charlotte put her bag down on one corner of the blanket to keep it from flying away.

"They are." He sat down, taking his backpack off. "I brought a bunch of stuff, so hopefully I've found something that's a hit."

He laid out all of the food–fruit, three different kinds of crackers, four different kinds of cheese, hummus, carrots, charcuterie meats and bite-sized brownies.

"Wow, this all looks so great, thanks!" Charlotte eyed the spread and started to fill up her plate.

"So is Bruno like that other dog? Nervous at the clinic, but rambunctious at home?" Ethan asked, filling his plate too. "Though he's a very sweet dog, even when he's scared."

"Oh, he's full of energy, especially now that he has his cast off. He absolutely loves getting the biggest piece of driftwood possible and dragging it around." Charlotte laughed. "It looks ridiculous–let me show you a picture."

She pulled out her phone and showed him the video she'd taken of Bruno the other morning, trying and failing to pick up a huge piece of wood. Well, calling it a piece of wood was a stretch–it looked like a young tree that had washed ashore. Ethan snorted.

"He's very sure of himself."

"He really is." Charlotte put her phone away. "He tries to take on the ocean every time we go down to the beach, like he's going to win in a fight against it. I'm not sure what he's trying to accomplish, but he's trying his best every time. I don't want to break it to him that there's a lot more to the ocean than the waves that wash up on the beach."

Ethan's laughter shook his shoulders. "I love all animals, of course, but little things like that make dogs my favorite. Actually, I can't even say that for sure—all animals have something special about them."

"Which ones tend to surprise you the most?"

Ethan took a few moments to consider it, layering some cheese on a cracker. "Rats—domesticated ones, I mean. They're incredibly smart, but I don't get to work with them that often."

"Rats? Really?" Charlotte had to shudder, pulling out the six-pack of canned wine that she'd bought from her bag. "I had a rat problem in the first apartment I rented after I graduated from college, so I can't even think about them without horrible memories. I know they're different and all, but still."

"Yeah, they're great pets. But having lived in terrible apartment buildings in college, I don't blame you for not liking the kinds of rats that infest buildings," he said. "Is that wine in a can?"

"It is." Charlotte held a can out toward him. "I

hope that's fine—I just thought it would be convenient."

"It's great. I was just about to say that I like it for that very reason." He smiled and took the can.

"That's a total relief. I know next to nothing about wine so whatever's easy and delicious is exactly what I go for." She cracked her can open, as did Ethan. "Cheers?"

"Cheers." He tapped his can against hers and took a sip. "Wow, that's good. I mean, I'm also a bit clueless about wine but what tastes good, tastes good."

"Exactly." Charlotte shook her head and put her can down, grabbing a mini-brownie. "In my early twenties, I thought understanding wine was a thing a 'real adult' did. But then I realized that it was fine to just like what you like."

"It's freeing to realize that you don't have to care about what people think."

"Agreed."

Charlotte nibbled on her brownie, immediately thankful that it was small because it was so rich. Ethan went for more cheese and crackers as they sat in silence that felt comfortable at first before it got a tinge awkward.

"So, how was your week?" Ethan asked, obviously eager to keep the conversation flowing.

"Not bad! It's been a little busier at the bookstore lately, so I've been on my feet a lot." She wiggled her toes. "It's a relief to sit down. I bet you're on your feet a lot too."

"I am. It's a surprisingly physical job, even with cats and dogs. In medical school we had to deal with larger animals, and some days I felt like I'd run a marathon."

Ethan told stories about his time in vet school, loosening up any lingering awkwardness from their quiet moment. Once the music started, their conversation shifted to the pleasant folksy jazz and the other kinds of music they liked. As it turned out, they had a lot of favorite bands in common, though they had drastically different taste in TV shows.

The conversation flowed easily the rest of the night and she had a nice time, but Charlotte couldn't help but feel like something wasn't quite clicking. Ethan was good-looking, kind, and fun, plus he checked all of the other boxes Charlotte wanted—intelligent, hardworking, and laid back.

But looking at him didn't make her heart skip a beat, and she didn't find her thoughts drifting to him during the day. There wasn't that indescribable spark that she looked for in a date or potential relationship.

After the concert, they packed up and he drove her back. Charlotte swallowed, knowing what she had to do, as much as she dreaded it. She tried to think of how to tell him as Ethan walked her to her door.

"Thank you for tonight," Charlotte said, fiddling with her keys and not meeting his eye.

"Yeah, no problem. I had a really great time." Ethan smiled, tucking his hands into his pockets.

"I had a great time too, but I think it would be better if we hung out as friends next time." Charlotte bit her lip, and watched the mild disappointment appear in his eyes. "I'm sorry."

"Ah, I see. I understand. That would be nice too."

He gave her a gentle smile that said *no hard feelings*. The tension fell from her shoulders. Ethan really was a nice guy—he wouldn't have made a fuss at being rejected.

"Great." Charlotte heard some snuffling and snorting on the other side of the door, and quietly laughed. "It looks like Bruno wants to say hello—is that fine?"

"Yeah, more than fine." Ethan's face brightened again.

Charlotte unlocked the door and Bruno darted out, his tail whipping back and forth as he sniffed Charlotte, then Ethan, who kneeled down. Bruno was thrilled to see him, burying his face in his armpit before licking his chin. Ethan found Bruno's sweet spot right away—once he scratched him right above his tail, Bruno practically melted.

"Glad to see he's hopping around," Ethan said, standing back up.

"Yeah, he's at one hundred percent." Charlotte ran her hand over Bruno's head.

"Well, I should get going." Ethan gently squeezed Charlotte's upper arm, and Charlotte pulled him into a friendly hug. "I'm still glad we met."

"I'm glad we met too."

"I'll see you soon, then." He gave her one more smile before heading back to his car.

* * *

Briggs looked out the window and up the driveway, sighing and putting his wrench back in his tool belt. He couldn't stop messing with his tools or moving around, and had been antsy like that all day. Charlotte was still on her date with Ethan, and had been all afternoon. That was definitely part of why he felt so on edge.

But also, he was running out of projects. He'd fixed the porch, all the cracks in the walls, all the leaks, a broken windowsill, and countless other little things. Sure, he could have tinkered forever, getting ahead of potential problems or improving things that were already okay. It felt like Charlotte would have picked up on it if he did.

He sighed again, checking his watch, then looking back at the shelves he had been securing. They were built-in, a great feature, and he had secured a few of the shelves so they could hold more books. He hadn't really needed to fix the shelving, though Charlotte did have a lot of books, but he'd felt compelled to do it just to fill up his time. He had done something similar in the living room, where he had refinished part of the hardwood floor that looked a little duller than the rest, and repainted a few spots on the wall that had been scuffed.

He looked around again, debating whether to start something else. There was no use. The day was ending and he was starting to get hungry. He headed back to the guest house and started putting together a simple dinner, getting lost in his thoughts instead of listening to music as he usually did.

Leaving was usually easy for him, even though he often made friends wherever he stopped. There were a lot of ways to keep in touch if he wanted to, so walking away hardly made him blink. He thought he'd do the same this time around—finish up Charlotte's house, pack up, and keep driving south. But now he was realizing that the thought of filling up his bags, clearing out the little kitchenette that he'd fixed up, and moving on again wasn't appealing. He would have felt as if he were leaving something behind that he couldn't get back with a quick phone call or email.

For the first time in a long time, he wanted to stay.

Once she was inside, Charlotte kicked off her sandals and went to change into leggings and a t-shirt. Even though her outfit had been comfortable, nothing beat her favorite sleep shirt, which was soft and perfectly worn in. Once she was in her cozy clothes, she dialed Nina, who wanted updates on how things went with Ethan.

"Hey!" Nina said, picking up on the second ring. "How'd your date go?"

"Right to it, huh?" Charlotte smiled, going back downstairs to get some water and stretch out on the couch.

"Well, it's exciting and he sounds nice. Sue me." Nina laughed.

"It was a really nice date. We went to this outdoor concert and had a little picnic, but the whole time I kept thinking that something was missing. It was just that feeling, you know? The spark," Charlotte said, stepping around Bruno to grab a glass. "So I told him that I just wanted to be friends when we got back."

"Oh, that's a bummer."

"Yeah, but it's better for me to tell him now than string him along. He took it really well, even though he looked pretty disappointed." Charlotte filled her glass, then headed into the living room. "We'll have to see each other again whenever I take Bruno to the vet, but I'm sure it'll be fine. He really is a great guy, but not for me."

"At least you gained a new friend."

"Yeah, exactly. That's always nice to have these days."

Charlotte stretched her legs out in front of her,

making a little space between her and the back of the couch so Bruno could jump up. As much as she wanted to keep him off the furniture, those big, sweet eyes of his melted her heart. He had been especially comforting since she discovered what had happened between Jean and her mother. It took him a moment to get settled in his spot, but soon he rested his head on her thigh and sighed.

"It sounds like everything went just fine—what's on your mind?" Nina asked.

"I found one of Jean's diaries and read it." Charlotte absently stroked Bruno's head. "It's been a lot to process."

"You have? What's in it?"

"Stuff about her life, of course, and something big." Charlotte swallowed, then. "Dad was in love with her, and she told him that she didn't feel the same—she was in love with another man. She wasn't sure how to tell Mom, but she didn't have to. Mom overheard him telling Jean how he felt again and everything fell apart."

"Wow." Nina went quiet for a moment. "That's insane.

"I know. Now a lot of things make more sense." Charlotte sighed.

"Yeah." Nina sighed too. "I can't believe Mom

kept all of that from us even as adults. Even after Jean passed away."

"Really?" Charlotte's brows furrowed. "I believe it. I doubt Mom would want to reveal such a terrible part of her life, even though we should have known. Since when has she done anything with a hair out of place?"

"Okay, true. It just stinks to find out this way, even though I appreciate knowing." Nina yawned. "I've got to go get ready for bed since I have an early morning tomorrow. Talk soon."

"Bye."

Charlotte hung up, putting her phone down on her thigh. She felt a little bit lighter having told Nina about the situation with Jean, like she wasn't carrying this burden all on her own They confided in each other all the time, and she knew Nina could understand her feelings like no one else could.

Suddenly, Bruno's ears perked up, then there was a noise in the kitchen.

Charlotte froze, her heart racing in her chest. Was it a burglar? She couldn't remember whether she'd closed all of the windows or locked all the doors. Sea Breeze Cove was safe, but nowhere was entirely free from break-ins.

Bruno hopped off the couch, fully alert but

sticking next to Charlotte's side. The closest, heaviest object she could find was a huge rooster figurine that she had found so ridiculous that she'd kept it. Hopefully it was going to come in handy.

She snuck into the kitchen, holding the rooster out in front of her and hoping she didn't have to use it. Then, she flipped on a light and shrieked.

Right in the middle of the floor, there was a huge raccoon, who looked just as shocked to see her as she was shocked to see it. It had a banana in one of its little paws, but that didn't slow it down from making a break for it around the counter and hopefully out of the house.

"Charlotte?" Briggs threw the door open, looking around with his eyes wide. "Are you okay?"

Charlotte started laughing, putting the rooster down on the counter. The quick rise and fall of her adrenaline somehow made her laugh harder, pressing her hand to her chest to calm her heart.

"What happened?" Briggs asked, still concerned.

"It was a raccoon, right here in the middle of the kitchen," Charlotte said, catching her breath. "I thought it was a burglar, so I brought this rooster as a weapon. How ridiculous would it have been if I threw this thing at a raccoon?"

Tension fell from Briggs's shoulders and he

chuckled. "That would have been pretty ridiculous, but it would make for a funny story. It doesn't help that they always look surprised, which makes it an even sillier situation."

"I've never seen a raccoon in real life! It was so big and it looked like it had little hands. He even stole a banana." Charlotte shook her head. "A banana, of all things."

"Yeah, their little paws look like that. If he got into the fridge, we'd have a mess on our hands. How'd he get in?"

"I have no idea. Maybe he just opened the door and strolled right in."

"Hm." Briggs walked around a little, a little smile on his face. "Ah, here we go—the window screen over here is torn."

Charlotte went around and examined the spot, standing next to Briggs. The window had been open, and Briggs closed it.

"He must have been hungry," she said.

"Yeah, or he just smelled something and decided to be ambitious." Briggs shrugged. "I'll fix it first thing tomorrow."

"Thank you," Charlotte said quietly.

Charlotte looked up at Briggs, suddenly realizing how close together they were standing. She hadn't intended to, but it felt right after the panic that had torn through her when she first heard the noise in the kitchen.

She could sense his body heat, they were that close together, and smell his shampoo. His hair looked slightly damp, like he'd taken a shower not long ago. Their gazes caught, and something sent a warm shiver up Charlotte's spine.

She wasn't sure who went for the kiss first, her or Briggs, but it didn't matter. There was that indescribable feeling right away, warm and tingly, racing from where their lips met to the tips of her fingers and toes. Briggs laced his fingers in hers, giving them a gentle squeeze, almost as if he were trying to reassure her that this was really happening. The contrast between the rough skin of his hands and the gentleness of his touch made Charlotte melt even more.

Everything about it felt right. This was the spark that she had been missing.

CHAPTER EIGHTEEN

Briggs felt so good having Charlotte in his arms, her small hand warm in his. She was a perfect fit, tucking herself under his chin so he could smell the sea salt in her auburn hair. As hard as he'd tried to keep his walls up around her, he couldn't anymore.

There was no way he could deny how he felt for her after he heard her yelp and sprinted over without a second thought. The idea of her being hurt or someone breaking into her home scared him to his core. He really cared about her, more than he ever dreamed he would.

He lifted her chin and gave her another brief kiss, making her sigh softly. She looked into his eyes, a gentle smile in hers.

"Are you tired?" he asked.

"Not in the slightest. I think the adrenaline from tonight is going to keep me up." Charlotte chuckled. "Who knew that raccoon break-ins were the best energy boost out there?"

"Yeah, who knew? And good," Briggs said with a grin. "Because I'm not tired either."

* * *

They walked along the empty beach, which was illuminated by moonlight. Bruno, excited to be back in the sand, romped in front of them, sniffing pieces of driftwood and tufts of grass. Charlotte was barefoot in her leggings and t-shirt, which was fine in the house but a little too bare on the breezy beach.

"Cold?" Briggs asked, putting his arm around her.

"Yeah, just a bit. It's breezy." She leaned into him, absorbing his warmth from his flannel shirt. He had a blanket under his other arm, but this was much better. Briggs smelled like grass and the salt from the ocean, and his side felt solid, steadying her.

They walked in comfortable silence for a bit. It was funny how easily they could talk, and how easily they could just be next to each other, like they could be comfortable just as they were. When Charlotte looked up at Briggs, she could tell that he was debating something in his head. She let him think it over, and soon he spoke.

"I've been moving around a lot ever since my wife and son died a few years back," he said quietly.

"I'm sorry to hear that," Charlotte said just as quietly. She had an initial flash of surprise, but then it started to make sense. This must have been why he was so guarded.

"Thank you." He paused for a few moments, but Charlotte didn't want to interrupt with any questions. "They died in a car crash—a reckless driver. We settled out of court since it was the other driver's fault, and I got a settlement. I know it's supposed to be some sort of compensation, but it isn't, not really. I put that money into a savings account and haven't touched it."

Charlotte could completely understand that. Money helped with concrete things, but nothing could replace family or loved ones.

Briggs pulled Charlotte a little bit closer, almost unconsciously, and looked off into the distance in front of them.

"I was up in Bangor for about six months before this, then a bunch of places before that. Made a few friends, then moved on before they could ask a lot of questions. It feels like I've been running away from grief. Whenever I settle in a place too long, I feel it more for some reason," he said. "Want to sit here?"

"Yeah, sure."

Charlotte helped him put the blanket down and sat next to him, her side pressed to his. He put his arm around her again to keep her warm.

"I think I've felt like settling down would mean that I was at risk of hurting like that again. Like my brain just doesn't want to let me settle and create a new home." He tilted his head to the side. "Does that make sense?"

"It does. It makes a lot of sense." Charlotte rested her hand on his. "That kind of loss is unthinkable, so no wonder you'd avoid anything that could lead to that. And having people you're attached to is home, like that old saying."

"Exactly. The idea of having a home base like I used to was so hard to wrap my mind around for a long time, and then moving from place to place had just become a habit, almost." His eyes warmed, like even more of his walls were coming down. "But now I feel like staying put for the first time in a long time."

He gave Charlotte a brief kiss on the forehead as she soaked in everything that he had just told her—it was more than she'd ever learned about him before, and the fact that he'd shared this meant so much to her. It was hard to imagine just how devastating something like that would be, and revisiting it wasn't easy. She linked her fingers in his, feeling the dampness of his palms that hadn't been there before.

He'd lost everything that was home to him, so it was no wonder that he didn't want to create a new home and have that taken away too. Her heart broke for him. He was such a kind man and didn't deserve any of the misery he had experienced.

"Thank you for telling me, Briggs," Charlotte said. "I know it can't have been an easy thing to share."

"You're really easy to talk to. I can practically feel you listening." The corners of his mouth lifted into a slight smile. "I hadn't been expecting that when we first met. Well, met and had a proper conversation instead of just getting your car out of the sand."

"I wasn't expecting it either." Charlotte smiled too. "But I'm not sorry I found it."

She went to give him a kiss again, but Bruno poked his head between them, almost like he was trying to climb into both their laps. They laughed, petting him instead.

CHAPTER NINETEEN

Sunday mornings were usually Addison's time to recharge. Jesse was often at the auto shop, taking care of customers who needed their cars fixed before the work week, so she and Lainey could play and spend time together. Most Sundays they played dress-up, creating a huge pile of costumes in the middle of Lainey's bedroom floor, but other times, like today, they stayed in the living room and energetically acted out whatever Lainey's creative brain had dreamed up.

But today, even after a cup of coffee and a surprisingly long night of rest, Addison felt like she was barely awake enough to make it through the morning, much less the rest of the afternoon.

Maybe it was the pancakes—she had put a little

extra syrup on them, but that usually didn't make her feel like she could curl up and sleep for a year after the sugar rush wore off. And the coffee was definitely caffeinated since Jesse had had a cup of it too. Despite all the cream she put in hers, it wasn't sitting well in her stomach like it usually did.

Or maybe it was the quality of her sleep. Even though she had been down for eight hours, she woke up a few times after Jesse hogged the covers or made her overheat from cuddling. But that was almost always the case, and had been since they'd been together. It never made her feel like this.

"Mommy, it's Princess Coco's turn," Lainey said, nudging her stuffed cat against the doll that Addison had been holding.

"Oh, sorry." Addison blinked a few times, trying to remember what today's story was. Lainey made up the most off-the-wall scenarios for her toys to play out, so it was hard to remember what on earth she was supposed to do. "It's time for her to bungee jump, right?"

"Yeah." Lainey made her stuffed cat climb up onto the couch, and Addison followed suit.

As Addison made Princess Coco "bungee jump", something clicked in her head. This wasn't the first time she'd felt like this. She did some quick mental math, her heart fluttering at the possibility.

"Hold on just a second, honey," Addison said, getting up to grab her phone.

She shot a text to Sadie, Elise, and Charlotte, asking them to come over as soon as they could. There was no way she could handle this without a little extra support.

* * *

Charlotte hummed to herself as she poured herself another cup of coffee. She desperately needed it. As much as she wanted to sleep in, she didn't want to ruin her sleep schedule for the work week. She and Briggs were out so late on the beach that the sun was almost coming up when they got back. They talked about everything in their lives; Briggs opening up about his wife and son had blown down a wall between them.

She loved learning more about him. He told her about the dog that he had mentioned once, a mutt that he and his wife had adopted from a shelter named Reggie. Charlotte couldn't help but smile at the memory of how passionate he sounded about the construction business he had once owned. It made a lot of sense—he was incredibly organized and great at his job. Everything he told her helped her connect the dots.

And she opened up to him as well. She told him about Jean and what she had read in the diary, trusting him to keep the secret close to the vest, and about her life back in Chicago. They bonded over their mutual love of Chicago style pizza, home renovation shows, and classic rock.

She couldn't have asked for a better night. The feeling of being in sync with someone, but not so similar that things were boring, was one she had missed. Then again, she wondered if she had ever really felt like this in the past.

Her phone buzzed on the counter and she grabbed it—it was Addison, asking her to come over without explaining why. Charlotte replied, telling her she'd be right over. Whatever it was, it had to be important.

After quickly dressing and making sure that Bruno had his breakfast, Charlotte drove over to Addison's. Elise and Sadie were already there, so Charlotte parked behind them.

"Hey, thanks for coming on such short notice," Addison said breathlessly when she opened the door. Just as she had looked when she stopped by the bookstore, she was dressed a little haphazardly in leggings and a big gray t-shirt that read "Sea Breeze Cove Auto".

"Yeah, it's no problem!"

Charlotte stepped inside and followed Addison to the kitchen, where Sadie and Elise were sitting at the island. After giving them each a quick hug, Charlotte sat on a stool and looked around at her friends. Sadie and Elise looked equally in the dark as Charlotte felt.

"So, my period is late," Addison said, clutching a bag from the nearby pharmacy in front of her. "I think this might be it and I needed the moral support."

"Well, you definitely have it!" Elise said, going into her massive tote bag and pulling out a box. "And I brought donuts too, if you want some comfort food right now."

"I think I'm way too anxious to eat anything." Addison rested her hand on her stomach. "But I'll have one later. The one with chocolate sprinkles looks good."

"We'll definitely save a few for you," Charlotte said.

"Thank you, guys." Addison gave them a shaky smile. "I'm going to go take it."

"We'll be right here for you no matter what," Sadie added.

Addison slipped down the hallway to the bathroom. Charlotte, Sadie, and Elise dug into the donuts, a nervous energy in the air. No one even spoke. Instead, they dug into their donuts. They all downed their first one within minutes, and Sadie started on her second right away.

"How did you know to bring donuts, Elise?" Sadie asked.

"I don't know." Elise shrugged. "I could just tell that Addison was stressing out. She never sends cryptic texts like that."

Both Charlotte and Sadie nodded, and in doing so, Sadie bit down on her donut so hard that some jam went spilling over her fingers.

"Sorry, I'm a little nervous for both Addison and myself," Sadie said, delicately sucking a bit of jam off her thumb. "I'm going to apply for a loan to start my dog daycare business tomorrow. The appointment is made and everything."

"That's great, Sadie!" Charlotte said. "Stress eat all you want. That's a huge deal."

"Seriously." Elise nodded. "You've been wanting this for a long time. Congrats!"

Sadie smiled, fidgeting with a napkin. "Thanks, guys."

"What made you take the plunge?" Charlotte debated whether to take another donut, then stopped herself.

"I was wandering around in town and ended up talking to the owner of that new secondhand clothing shop," Sadie said. "She told me that her only regret was that she didn't take the dive into her business sooner, and that she was lucky to get the space that she was in. I figured, why wait? I know where I want it to be, but I just need to actually make it happen. I hope the space is still available."

"I hope it is too." Elise took another donut.

"Where is it?" Charlotte asked.

"It's over near the organic food store, right on the way into town." Sadie's nerves seemed to be replaced by excitement in an instant. "It's a perfect spot for my clients to drop off dogs on their way to work and it's far enough out of the thick of town to have a bunch of space for boarders and for dogs to run around both inside and outside."

"It sounds like it's meant to be!" Elise grinned. "How often does a space like that become available around here?"

They all turned toward the hallway when they heard the bathroom door open. Addison came down the hallway, stopping at the entrance to the kitchen and resting her hand on the wall. She was pale as a sheet.

"Hey, it's okay," Charlotte said softly.

"Yeah, it could still happen down the road." Elise slid off her chair, but hesitated as if she wasn't sure if Addison wanted a hug or not.

"No, it's not that. It's not bad news." Addison shook her head. "It's good news—I'm pregnant."

* * *

Briggs woke up feeling better than he had in a long time despite getting the fewest hours of sleep that he'd had since he came to Sea Breeze Cove. Luckily he only had to replace the screen where the raccoon had broken in last night, which didn't require a lot of energy. He had plenty of time to take a nap later if he wanted to, but he doubted he would—he was too happy.

It was as if a weight had been lifted off of his shoulders after years and years of carrying it. Kissing Charlotte and finally letting his walls down had felt just right, even though it was scary at first. But as they had started talking, the more he'd felt himself falling for everything about her from her big, warm smile to the quiet intensity in her eyes as she really listened to him. They'd talked for hours and hours after their kiss. Even his voice was a tiny bit hoarse—it was the longest, most in-depth conversation he'd had in ages.

He finished up the screen, gently pressing it to test it, and it held.

"Hopefully Charlotte won't have any more raccoon guests," Briggs said to Bruno, who had laid down next to him as he worked.

He heard a car pull up the driveway, and Briggs went to the front door to greet Charlotte, Bruno rushing ahead of him. But when he opened the door, he realized it was a car he didn't recognize. An older woman stepped out of the car, and as she approached, Briggs recognized who she had to be—Charlotte's mother.

CHAPTER TWENTY

Charlotte was so excited for Addison. She and Jesse had wanted another child for so long, and Charlotte knew Lainey would be excited to be a big sister when they told her the news. She would have another kid to help her act out her elaborate stories, at least when the baby got older.

Charlotte thought about the rest of her day and what she was going to do on the drive home—maybe relax with Briggs on the beach, or maybe they could have dinner together. He had talked about a great recipe he had for pork tenderloin that she was dying to try, but it was a little bit too warm for the oven. The ancient grill that had been out back wasn't working, to her chagrin.

But all of her plans went up in smoke when she

came inside and saw her mother sitting on the couch, looking put together as always. She was wearing a sand-colored linen dress that somehow hadn't wrinkled, and her hair was in its usual neat chignon.

"Mom?" Charlotte blinked a few times. It felt as if she'd come for a surprise inspection of her and the house. Thankfully things looked and felt much better than they had when she arrived.

"Hi, Charlotte." Melissa got up and hugged her daughter. "Briggs let me in."

"Hey," Briggs said, coming out of the kitchen with a glass of water. He handed it to Melissa, who thanked him.

There was a brief awkward pause. Charlotte had no idea how to proceed, and was still trying to process the fact that her mom was even there. It was so odd seeing Briggs, who was tied to Sea Breeze Cove, next to her mother, who she hadn't seen in this town in over a decade.

"So...you said you were a handyman?" Melissa asked, looking between Briggs and Charlotte as she sipped her water

"Yeah, I am. I've been doing all the repairs on the house." Briggs gently rubbed the back of his neck and looked at Charlotte. "I'm living in the guest house and fixing that up too."

"He's..." Charlotte tried to shape what they were into words. It was surprisingly awkward even though being with him felt right. "We're seeing each other."

Briggs nodded with a little shrug. Charlotte had no idea what they were yet, at least officially. All she knew was that she really cared about him and that they had a connection that felt like it ran deep. Melissa's eyebrows went up in surprise.

"Oh. How nice," Melissa said with a polite smile.

"It's pretty recent," Charlotte added.

"Well, good for you both." Melissa looked out the front window. "I should probably get my bags inside —I don't want any of my makeup to get baked in that sun."

"Do you want help?" Briggs asked.

"No, no, I'm fine, but thank you for the offer." Melissa stood and waved him off. "I just have a small weekend bag since I'll be here for just a few days. I'll be back in a few moments."

Melissa went out to her car and Charlotte walked Briggs back to the guest house.

"I'm sorry," Charlotte said with a sigh. "This isn't how I imagined this day would go. I hope my mom didn't bombard you with questions."

"No, not at all. She was very polite."

Charlotte let out a slow breath and Briggs pulled her closer, his hands on her shoulders.

"I can handle your mom, Charlotte. Don't worry. " He smiled, then gave her a quick kiss on the lips before slipping inside.

* * *

Charlotte wished her mother had called first. Even though the guest bedroom was prepared, she hadn't gotten groceries or anything her mom liked to eat, and she hadn't planned anything fun to do. But Charlotte didn't get the sense that her mother had popped in by surprise for any negative reasons. She just wanted to see how Charlotte was. It was sweet, if overbearing.

The next morning, Charlotte got dressed for work and found Melissa in the kitchen making coffee and looking around. The kitchen had been in better shape than a lot of the other rooms, but it hadn't been particularly stylish when it was built and it definitely wasn't now.

It had old countertops that were scratched a bit from time, mismatched appliances, and a small amount of counter space. There were tiles instead of old linoleum, but they didn't quite go with the cabinets.

As much as Charlotte wanted to replace the countertop and tiles, she couldn't afford it. Instead, Briggs had given the cabinets a fresh coat of paint and replaced the old knobs with something newer, which had gone a long way toward improving how it looked. But it still had the same old-fashioned feeling that Charlotte remembered from childhood.

"Coffee's ready," Melissa said. "Where do you keep your mugs?"

"Up here." Charlotte grabbed two and put them on the counter. "Thanks for making coffee."

"Oh, no problem. You know how I can be without mine." Melissa smiled.

"Ah, I don't think I have cream or anything besides a bit of milk," Charlotte said, looking around the fridge. There were just some sad leftover potatoes that didn't add up to a full serving, some eggs, and some butter. "I really need to go to the store."

"It's fine. I'll drink mine with just a little sugar, if you have it. You can have the rest of the milk."

Charlotte did, and she pulled the sugar from the pantry. Once Melissa stirred her sugar in and

Charlotte topped her coffee off with milk, they enjoyed their drinks in peace for a few moments.

"What are you up to today?" Melissa asked, cupping her mug with both hands.

"I have to go to work for most of the day." Charlotte bit her lip. "I'm sorry."

"Don't apologize—I'm the one who showed up without warning." Melissa smiled over the rim of her mug. "Do you like it there so far?"

"I do! I love it. It brings me back to my days working at bookstores in college, but it's a lot more fun being there full-time and knowing a little bit more about the industry. Plus I'm working on setting up a writers' group too, so I can get back to mentoring other writers and maybe writing a little more myself again for fun."

"That's great! I'm glad you're getting back to writing. It seemed like your old job made you put a lot of energy into other people's writing for a while."

"It did, yeah. But it was really rewarding to see their already great writing grow," Charlotte said. "Do you want to come with me, actually? I'm sure my boss Daisy won't mind at all. I'll show you around town too.

Melissa hesitated for a few moments before saying, "Sure, that would be nice."

They headed to the bookstore and parked a little farther away than usual so Charlotte could show Melissa around. Charlotte sensed tension in her mother's shoulders from the moment they got out of the car, as much as Melissa tried to hide it.

"So, here's downtown. A lot of businesses have popped up lately, like this little boutique." Charlotte gestured toward the boutique, which had a few dresses in the window.

"Wow, it's been a long time since I've been in this area," Melissa said, looking around at all the shops. "It feels so different, but kind of the same."

Even though Melissa's tone was nostalgic, the tightness in her shoulders didn't go away. The store was quiet, but she still seemed stressed. That made more sense than ever to Charlotte now that she knew what memories probably came to mind when she was there. Every single place probably reminded Melissa of what had happened between her and Jean.

Charlotte was still shocked that her father had made a pass at Jean, and it erased any desire to forge a relationship with him now that she was older. He'd more or less dropped out of their lives when he and Melissa had divorced. Charlotte wanted to say something to Melissa about it, but where could she even start with something as big as that?

"And this place has amazing salads. I come here for lunch all the time when I want to eat a little healthier without sacrificing taste," Charlotte said instead, stopping outside a small, quaint eatery.

"It does look nice. It's like those little lunch places in Chicago." Melissa looked over the menu in the window. "There are a lot of restaurants now. I'm a little surprised."

"Yeah, I was too. We should go out for dinner later. My friend Elise's father owns a restaurant with the *best* seafood I've ever had, hands down. Or if you want something a little spicy, there's a fusion place with a bunch of dishes that are inspired by Thailand and New England."

"I'd love to try both while I'm here." The tension that Melissa had been carrying started to ease a bit until she spotted something up ahead. She didn't say anything about it. "And it would be nice to meet your friends. You said her name was Elise?"

"Yeah, Elise, Sadie, and Addison. Sadie has a dog-walking business and Addison has a sweet little five-year-old named Lainey," Charlotte said. "We met at a café where they invited me to book club, which led to me getting this job."

"Wow, that's a stroke of luck."

"It is."

"It seems like a lot of things are falling into place for you here." Melissa smiled, giving Charlotte a knowing look out of the corner of her eye. "Especially Briggs."

"Mom." Charlotte's cheeks heated up. She almost felt like she did in high school when she brought a boyfriend to dinner for the first time.

"What?" Melissa shrugged. "I'm just curious to know more about him. You two seem very fond of each other."

"We are." Charlotte's heart warmed as her initial embarrassment faded. "I'm sure you'll get a chance to talk to him more while you're here."

They chatted about a few other sites they passed until they arrived at The Book Nook. It was surprisingly quiet. Usually around this hour, Daisy was bustling about. A few customers looked up at her, obviously confused at how the shop was open, but no one was working at the counter. Charlotte frowned.

"Feel free to look around," Charlotte said almost absently as she headed toward the back.

She found Daisy in the back, kneeling on the floor next to a box of books and looking much paler than usual. Daisy hardly looked up at Charlotte, putting her hand to her chest, her face tense with pain. Charlotte's stomach dropped and she scrambled for her phone.

* * *

Sadie put on a song that always pumped her up as she drove to the bank. She finally had her appointment to speak to someone about her small business loan, and she needed all the positive vibes she could get. The dog daycare of her dreams was just one step closer.

She took a long, shaky breath. The person she was meeting with was extremely nice on the phone, but that didn't put Sadie at ease as much as she wanted to. What if the person laughed at her ideas, or found massive holes in the math she'd done to figure out how much she needed in her loan? Or what if she got denied? And even if she did get the loan, what if she had waited too long and the space she wanted was gone?

Her song and train of thought was interrupted by a phone call from Addison, which she answered.

"Hey, what's up?" Sadie asked.

"It's Daisy," Addison said, sounding anxious.

"She's having a heart attack. Charlotte called the ambulance and they rushed her over to the hospital."

"A heart attack? Daisy? When?" Sadie slowed down a little, gripping the steering wheel.

The thought of Daisy being in pain was terrifying—she had always been so vivacious and bubbly. Even though she was getting older, Sadie never thought anything like this would happen so suddenly.

"Not too long ago. I bet she just got to the hospital in the ambulance. Charlotte was the one who found her, and just in time it seems."

"I can't believe this," Sadie said. "I'll be there soon, okay?"

"See you soon."

Sadie made a U-turn and headed back the way she came. She had to be there for Daisy—she was a regular fixture in Sadie's life because of the book club, and Daisy was one of the sweetest women she had ever met.

Sadie made it to the hospital after a streak of green lights, and rushed inside to find Charlotte, Addison, and Elise in the waiting area. They all hugged, squeezing each other extra tight.

"Is there any news?" Sadie asked.

"She had some sort of heart incident, but it was

minor. The doctors are running tests," Charlotte said, crossing her arms as if she were hugging herself. "Also, sorry—I should introduce you to my mom Melissa. Mom, this is my friend Sadie."

A woman who looked a little like Charlotte, with a put-together air about her, stepped into view.

"Lovely to meet you, Sadie," Melissa said.

"Likewise. I wish it were under better circumstances." Sadie tried to smile, but couldn't.

Charlotte looked past Sadie's shoulder, her eyes lighting up ever so slightly. It was Briggs.

"Hey, you made it," Charlotte said, meeting him halfway.

He pulled her into his arms and gave her a kiss on the forehead. Addison and Sadie looked at Elise, their eyes wide, but Sadie wasn't surprised—she was just a little pleased that her gut instinct was right. She'd had a feeling that Charlotte had a thing for Briggs for a while now.

Any time Charlotte said his name, even if she was just talking about pulling up weeds or fixing a toilet, her face softened a little bit. Once she had come over to Charlotte's so they could walk on the beach with Bruno and their eyes had seemed to follow each other whenever Briggs was near. Seeing him comfort her now, it was clear that things had become real between them.

Sadie didn't have time for love at the moment, what with her business dreams finally becoming a reality, but that didn't stop her heart from warming at the display. It was a touch of sweetness in a dark situation.

Wouldn't it be nice to have someone care for me like that? She thought.

CHAPTER TWENTY-ONE

Daisy sighed as the nurse poked and prodded at the machines she was hooked up to. She felt like a pincushion, but it was better to be thorough, she supposed. Before this happened, her doctor had gently warned her to be more mindful of her heart health after running some tests, but Daisy had thought she had it under control. She was active with the store, had a lot of great friends, and was eating a healthier diet than she ever had.

But stress. That was the one piece of advice from her doctor that she had a hard time following. Maybe part of it was stubbornness—she didn't like the idea of having to slow down even though her mind was still sharp. But another part was probably just the way her life was set up. Charlotte had lightened her workload significantly, but maybe the damage had already been done.

Daisy sighed. Even though she was embarrassed at how Charlotte had found her, she was grateful that she had arrived when she did. The pain had been so severe that she hadn't been able to cry out for help. If Charlotte hadn't arrived at that moment... Daisy shuddered. She was thankful to be safe in the hospital and for all of her friends who were in the waiting room.

"Alright, we'll let you rest," the nurse said with a smile. "Don't hesitate to press that button if you need anything."

"Thank you." Daisy smiled.

"Oh, it looks like you have guests!" the nurse called over her shoulder. "Go ahead, ladies."

Daisy smiled as she saw Sadie, Elise, Charlotte, and Addison come in, holding a vase of daisies. They all looked relieved to see her there.

"Hey, Daisy! We thought these were appropriate," Addison said, putting the flowers on the windowsill.

"Thank you all for being so sweet," Daisy said. "I love daisies, and not just because I'm named after them."

Everyone laughed.

"Have other people you've met who are named after flowers hated their namesakes?" Charlotte asked, adjusting the flower arrangement a little.

"Mm, not all of them. I did know a woman named Rose decades ago who refused a gorgeous bouquet of the prettiest roses you've ever seen, just because she was so tired of getting them." Daisy shook her head. "She had a lot of suitors, so she probably got a bouquet at least once a week."

"How are you feeling?" Elise asked. "Did the doctors say anything else?"

"Better than I look, I hope. There are so many machines and whatnot connected to me." Daisy shrugged. "They're still running the results, but the doctors think it was pretty minor. Seeing all of you has really made things better."

"You'll be out of here in no time," Sadie said.

"I hope so. I didn't even bring a book! I never go anywhere without one and of course, now that I have time to sit around for once, I don't have one." Daisy sighed.

"I have one you can borrow!" Charlotte dug into her purse and pulled out a paperback. "It's a mystery and I'm really loving it so far."

"You're amazing, thank you!" Daisy took the book and looked at the back cover.

They chatted for a little while longer until there was another knock on the door—Arthur, Elise's father.

"Sorry to interrupt," he said. "I just wanted to check-in on Daisy while I had a free moment."

"No worries. I think we all have to get going," Elise said, giving her dad a quick hug. "See you later."

Everyone else said their goodbyes and cleared out, leaving Arthur and Daisy alone. They had been friends for a long time—business owners in town were a close-knit community, though their friendship had gone beyond talking shop. He was a great sounding board for all of her ideas, and it didn't hurt that they usually met over a delicious meal. Daisy felt like he understood her, and she understood him.

Their businesses weren't just ways to build an income—they were their lives. In the decades since they had each started with just a little money, passion, and ideas, they had both poured all of their energy into the work, even when it was inconvenient. Daisy felt like her whole identity was tied up in the shop in some ways, but now she was seeing just how detrimental that could be. It was keeping her from doing what was best for her health.

"It's so good to see you," Arthur said, worry

written all over his face. "When Elise told me you were in the hospital I had to come see you. I could hardly believe it."

"Neither can I. It's like my brain is still young, but my body doesn't agree." Daisy sighed.

"Yeah, we aren't exactly spring chickens anymore." Arthur leaned against the windowsill next to the vase of daisies.

"What an old man expression," Daisy said with a laugh.

"Well, it fits." Arthur smiled. "How are you feeling?"

"Much better than earlier. The doctors here have really taken good care of me." Daisy lifted her arm. "But I can't wait until all these tests are done. I've been poked so many times with needles and sensors and whatnot that I feel like a science experiment."

"Have they told you what happened?" Arthur rubbed at his chin, his expression serious.

"It was a minor heart attack, or at least, the doctor is eighty percent sure it's that. Hopefully there isn't anything else." Daisy looked at the IVs and monitors she was hooked up to. "Well, besides a little dehydration but that's no big deal."

"It's good that they caught you just in time."

"Agreed. I was really lucky that Charlotte came

in just then. This all really puts things into perspective," Daisy said, lacing her fingers together in front of her. "I love my bookstore, but I want to enjoy these years instead of letting them fly by. Maybe working, working, working isn't the way to do that."

Arthur paused, considering her words. She could sense a bit of skepticism, but then he nodded. "That's true. Some days I look up and realize that a whole month has gone by before I knew it."

Daisy knew the feeling well. While Charlotte's help had given her a little more free time, she wasn't able to fully let go. Plus, she loved going into the shop. Talking about books with people, feeling the joy of someone learning to love reading for the first time or after a long time, and seeing regular customers week after week...it was such a regular occurrence to her that she had a hard time imagining what life would be like without it.

She and Arthur sat in comfortable silence as Daisy continued to think of what life would be like if she didn't push herself every single day. Scary, yes. Her entire routine rotated around getting coffee near her shop, opening, and making sure everything was ready for customers.

But it had been scary opening up her business

too, and she had made it thrive over time. She figured she would eventually find her footing if she slowed down too.

"Let's make a deal," Daisy said. "I'll stop and smell the roses if you will."

Arthur's eyebrows went up. "Really?"

"Yes, really." Daisy chuckled. "If I don't do it now from this hospital bed, when will I?"

Arthur smiled, and extended his hand to her. "I'll take you up on that deal."

* * *

Arthur stepped into the waiting room, where everyone was still lingering a little, and put a hand on Charlotte's shoulder. Something in his step and energy seemed a bit different than before, like he'd changed. Before Charlotte could say anything, he spoke.

"Daisy wants to speak with you," he said.

"Oh, okay." Charlotte's brows furrowed a little bit, and she went back into Daisy's room. "Hi again."

"Hi there." Daisy smiled. "Come, sit."

Charlotte settled into the chair next to Daisy's bed, worry filling her again. It was still so strange to see Daisy like this, a little tired instead of vibrant and excited about everything. Daisy had been a huge part of why her time in Sea Breeze Cove had been so amazing.

She'd never had a boss who was so warm and happy to listen. Even working at a publisher, she had never met anyone as enthusiastic about books as Daisy was, and that was saying something. Daisy could have found a book that even the most reluctant reader would love.

"Are you still okay?" Charlotte asked.

"I'll be fine, I promise." Daisy grinned. "I've already gotten a little of my spunk back."

"I'm so glad to hear it."

Daisy already did look better, like more color had come to her cheeks. Whatever she and Arthur discussed must have rejuvenated her.

"I brought you back in since I've made a tough decision." Daisy's expression fell a little. I'm closing the bookstore and selling the building. I have some money saved up for retirement that I've been sitting on for a while, but selling the building will let me fully retire now, and this whole situation has made me realize I need to just go for it. I made a promise to a friend that I'd slow down, too."

"Oh, wow, Daisy. That's a big decision,"

Charlotte said, swallowing the abrupt tightness in her throat.

Part of her knew that Daisy would slow down, but hearing that she was closing the shop was a genuine shock. The store was everything to Daisy, and she had run it for so long. Plus, the shop meant so much to the community. It was a place where book club met, of course, but it was also the only space that held book signings in the area. The children's read-along was popular among parents in the area, including Addison, Jesse, and Lainey.

Sea Breeze Cove wasn't going to be the same. But if that meant having Daisy around and happy, Charlotte could support her decision.

"I know. It wasn't a decision I made lightly. But it's definitely time. This whole incident has showed me that." Daisy reached for Charlotte's hand, and Charlotte took it. "But of course, that means you're out of a job. I'm really sorry."

"It's okay." Charlotte gently squeezed Daisy's hand. "I'm behind you one hundred percent, no matter what you do."

* * *

Later that afternoon, Charlotte finally stepped out of the hospital with Melissa and Briggs. She felt worn out from the day's events, from the spike in adrenaline of finding Daisy at the store, to the relief that she was okay, to the realization that she was out of a job again.

Still, her stomach growled.

"Want to get something to eat?" Briggs asked, resting a hand on Charlotte's back.

"Yeah, that would be good." Charlotte leaned into his touch a little bit. "Do you want something, Mom? Maybe that Thai fusion place I mentioned this morning?"

"Why don't you pick?" Melissa suggested gently. "Maybe some comfort food?"

"There's a great place not too far from here that I passed." Briggs gave her waist a squeeze. "Let's try it."

"That sounds good to me."

Briggs took them to the restaurant, which looked as cozy as the menu suggested the food was. They got a booth in the back, where Briggs and Charlotte sat on one side and Melissa sat on the other.

Charlotte looked over the menu, unsure of what she wanted. Something inside her wanted soup even though it was warm out, but all of the entrees, a mix of traditional comfort foods and lighter fare, were calling her name.

"Want to split something?" Briggs asked, as if reading her mind.

"That would be nice. Maybe the lobster macaroni and cheese, plus a salad?" Charlotte glanced up at her mother to see if she was interested in splitting anything. She shook her head.

"I'll just get a wrap—pick whatever you two would like." Melissa smiled.

"Okay, lobster mac and cheese, and a salad it is," Briggs said. He looked up and got the waiter's attention with a polite smile.

They ordered, adding on a bottle of white wine, and were left alone. Charlotte could sense Melissa studying her, then Briggs, then her again. *Uh-oh*, Charlotte thought. She could easily tell where Melissa's mind was going.

"So, Briggs. How did you and Charlotte meet, again?" Melissa asked, wrapping her hands around her glass of water.

"By chance. Twice." Briggs looked at Charlotte. "The first time, I helped her get her car out of the sand on the side of the road, but the second time, I answered the ad to help her fix up her house."

"I was pretty shocked when I saw him again." Charlotte chuckled. "But it was a stroke of luck."

Briggs smiled at Charlotte, temporarily distracting her from the very real fact that Melissa was probably going to pepper Briggs with questions. She had done the same thing with Peter when Charlotte first introduced him to her. Peter had done well enough, though Melissa hadn't been sure about how much backbone he had or what his job prospects were. As it turned out, she was right on both accounts.

But still, she didn't want Melissa to push Briggs too much. He had just opened up about his past to her and likely wasn't ready to do it in front of her mom.

"And you're a handyman?" Melissa sipped her water, not taking her eyes off of Briggs.

"I am, and a carpenter. I've done contractor work in the past too." Briggs sipped his water as well.

Melissa seemed pleased by that answer, to Charlotte's surprise. In the past, Melissa had gently suggested that she wanted Charlotte to date a doctor or lawyer or some other white collar career.

"You've done a lovely job on the house." Melissa paused as the waiter dropped off their wine, thanking him before he left. She raised her glass. "To Daisy's recovery?"

"Perfect," Charlotte said, clinking her glass against Melissa's.

"Anyway, yes, the house. It looks great." Melissa smiled.

"Thank you. A lot of that is thanks to Charlotte's organizing. It looks like a totally different house." Briggs gave Charlotte a proud smile.

"That too." Melissa's expression softened a little bit. "I can't even tell a dog lives there."

Charlotte laughed, leaning back in the booth. "Mom, not all dogs are little balls of chaos. Bruno just loves to cuddle, eat food, and play on the beach."

"I know, I know," Melissa said with a gentle smile.

"Briggs really helped me with Bruno as well. I don't know if I would have been able to get him to the vet if it wasn't for him." Charlotte couldn't help but feel warmth spread through her chest. Briggs and Bruno were close buddies, goofing around in ways that Charlotte and Bruno didn't. It was hilarious to watch them. Bruno absolutely loved playing tug of war and trying to catch balls that Briggs tossed.

"Ah, you're a dog person?" Melissa asked Briggs.

"I am. I've had dogs in the past." Briggs gently

swirled his wine. "There's nothing like coming home to an excited dog. And it's nice spending time with him and Charlotte, just walking on the beach."

Briggs put his arm around the back of the booth, and Melissa nodded, pleased with the answer. The silence that fell over the table made Charlotte a little nervous. So far, things were going well even though they were keeping things at a surface level. Were things going to go wrong, or was Charlotte just feeling anxious?

"And you've been successful with your handyman business?" Melissa asked, a little more suspicion in her tone.

"Mom," Charlotte said with a groan.

"It's alright, Charlotte." Briggs let his arm rest across Charlotte's shoulders. "It's a reasonable question. But yes, I've been pretty successful. I pride myself on doing good work and providing fair prices for everyone. It's very rewarding to me. Plus, it eventually led me to Charlotte."

Melissa's smile broadened wider than it had all day, and she looked to Charlotte. Any worries Melissa was going to dislike Briggs disappeared. If there was anything that Melissa liked, it was someone who worked hard and did work well. It was a trait that she had passed to Charlotte and Nina.

Briggs looked at Charlotte, unaware of how much those simple words had made an impact.

"So, have you been enjoying your visit so far?" Briggs asked Melissa. "We've been talking about me a lot but I haven't gotten to hear how you've been."

When Melissa launched into her experience on her trip, Charlotte felt more at ease than she had all day. She was so happy that she'd found Briggs and that her mother saw the good, hardworking man she saw too.

CHAPTER TWENTY-TWO

Melissa held the door open for Charlotte as they walked into a little cafe for breakfast, Melissa's treat. The Book Nook was officially closed down, so Charlotte didn't have much on her to-do list besides sprucing up her resume again. Her last paycheck from the bookstore was going to land in her bank account in a few days, but after that, everything felt unsure.

Melissa ordered a skim latte and a morning glory muffin, and Charlotte went for a mocha and an everything bagel with extra cream cheese as a comforting treat. Even though she was fully supportive of Daisy's decision, Charlotte was still a little stressed at the idea of finding a new job.

She tried to think of the positives. A lot of her

publishing skills could be applied to other areas, like marketing or copywriting. She had great recommendations, too. Her friends were more than willing to keep an ear out for any open jobs.

But still, it was scary to be back at square one again. She had no idea what other opportunities there were in town, or if she'd have to commute to a nearby city to find something.

"Are you feeling better today?" Melissa asked, sipping her latte. Last night had been rough for Charlotte now that the reality of her situation was fully hitting her.

"Yeah, a bit. I feel better now that Daisy has been discharged from the hospital, but I'm still not sure where to start on my job hunt." Charlotte blew across the top of her mug to cool her mocha. "I really lucked out with the job at The Book Nook. I was in the right place at the right time."

Melissa studied Charlotte, her eyes filled with concern. Charlotte hated to make her worry. This quick weekend trip had been anything but relaxing or refreshing. But to Melissa's credit, she hadn't shown a hint of displeasure.

"Maybe it's a good opportunity to move back to Chicago," Melissa said. "There are a lot more jobs there."

Charlotte sighed, looking out the window at the bustling street. "Bustling" for Sea Breeze Cove was far different than bustling back in Chicago. People walked at an easier pace, taking the time to smile at strangers and say hello. No one seemed to be annoyed that they had to be outside, especially not in weather like this.

"I don't know, Mom." Charlotte took a sip of her mocha, the sweet blend of chocolate and coffee warming her from the inside out.

"You wouldn't want to get back into publishing? I thought you loved your old job." Melissa's neatly shaped eyebrows furrowed.

"I did. I loved helping authors and the excitement of their books being published. But at The Book Nook, I was able to connect with readers again, especially people with no connections to the industry."

"And there's not another bookstore nearby?

"Not ones that are hiring, no."

"Then think bigger than this small town, Char." Melissa gently nudged her knee against Charlotte's. "There's a lot out there that could be a great fit. You can keep the house, of course–it could be a good source of extra income if you find good renters."

"I know." Charlotte smiled, trying to put her

mother at ease. "Just give me a little more time to process everything, okay?"

Melissa nodded, though the concern was still in her eyes. Charlotte could tell she wanted to push more, but thankfully she backed off.

The thoughts of what Charlotte had to do weighed on her mind as she and Melissa finished breakfast, took a quick walk, and did a little window shopping.

What did Charlotte really want in life? At first she'd come here to get away, recover from the double blow of losing her job and her ex, and figure out her next moves. Staying hadn't seriously crossed her mind back then.

But now, it did. She couldn't imagine *not* being here, waking up to the sound of waves crashing on the beach instead of traffic, getting dinner with her friends, and taking it slow for once.

Later, after she and Melissa got back to the house, Briggs stopped by. Bruno rushed to the door, his tail wagging furiously, and Briggs laughed, petting him.

"Want to go on a walk?" Briggs asked.

"Yeah, I'd love to." She needed to clear her head.

"I'm going to lie down for a little bit. You two have fun," Melissa said. Charlotte was a little grateful. As much as her mom liked Briggs, she wanted a little time alone with him.

They headed out, Bruno in front of them. The dog played in the surf, his tail wagging non-stop.

"He loves the water, doesn't he?" Briggs said, sliding an arm around Charlotte's waist.

"Definitely. I don't think he'll ever get tired of it." Charlotte cocked her head to the side, still studying the dog. "He never tries to swim, though."

"Ah, yeah. Maybe it's too cold. And maybe it's for the best." Briggs shrugged. "He might love it a little too much and refuse to come inside."

"He would definitely be sleepy enough for a long nap, though." Charlotte smiled.

Charlotte leaned against him as they continued to walk. With the sun shining overhead, the sand soft under their feet, it felt like a perfect moment. Bruno stopped for a moment, picking up a little driftwood and bringing it to Charlotte and Briggs. The dog wasn't great at fetch, but he tried his best, sprinting after the stick once Briggs threw it. They came to a stop, waiting for Bruno to get the stick.

Briggs slid his other arm around Charlotte, pulling her close and making Charlotte look up into his blue eyes. After they'd confessed their feelings for each other and opened up that night, there was a softness to Briggs's gaze when he looked at her that made the moment even better. He was still the same handsome man who had helped her when he could have just driven by, but now she saw the man he was deep inside—kind, gentle, and fun.

"Briggs, this has been the best summer I've ever had," Charlotte said quietly. Briggs rested his chin on the top of her head, making a small, pleased sound. "And I know you never stay in any one place for long, and I might not stay either. I'll always be glad I met you, no matter what happens."

Briggs tilted her head up and kissed her softly before pulling her even closer. The softness of his shirt against her cheek was comforting and the sound of his heart beating was calming, as always. He didn't say anything, though Charlotte felt the tenderness in his kiss. The walk back was equally as quiet, but not for lack of anything to say. Something was on his mind.

Charlotte bit her lip. Maybe it was a sign that this was the end, like he was trying to figure out a way to let her down easily. Part of her wondered if Briggs would be the type of guy to string her along, but she shut down that thought right away. He wasn't Peter by any stretch of the imagination.

If he was going to end their relationship, he'd tell

her directly without letting things drag out. They would go their separate ways with just the memories of this summer. The thought made her heart ache, but knowing why Briggs moved around a lot, she never wanted to make him stay. Even though he seemed like he'd addressed some of the things that kept him bouncing around to different towns, that didn't mean he wanted to anchor himself here.

Maybe her mother was right in telling her that this was a good opportunity to move back to Chicago. Without Briggs here, things wouldn't feel the same. She couldn't imagine how it would feel to walk along the beach with Bruno alone, or to not chat with Briggs over dinner, drinking wine and laughing until the sun went down. Losing her job might have been a sign that she needed to take heed of.

Soon they arrived back at the house, Bruno trotting alongside them. Charlotte was about to invite Briggs in for something to drink when he stopped.

"I need to go take care of some things," he said, squeezing her arm and giving her a soft kiss. "Be back later."

Charlotte watched him head to his truck, wondering what he had sorted out in his head on their walk.

* * *

Briggs took a deep breath as he pulled onto the main road, feeling filled with determination as he thought about what Charlotte had said. This had been the best summer he'd ever had in recent memory too.

There was only one thing he could do, knowing how Charlotte felt. He needed to move on from the heartbreak in his past, to let go of the grief that had been his only companion for so long.

He needed to try to do what had once been unthinkable to him: to allow himself to be happy again.

His beloved wife had always told him to find the joy in life, and he had lost sight of that in the years since she and their son had died. But he wasn't honoring their memories by living a half life himself.

It was time to put roots down again, and he knew exactly where he wanted to do that—and who he wanted to do it with.

He just had to take care of one little thing first.

* * *

Charlotte came inside to find Melissa sitting on the couch, reading a book. Charlotte felt a little pang of sadness in her chest. The book was one that she had recommended to basically every regular to the shop who loved historical romance. Her mother looked up at her with a gentle smile.

"Did you all have a nice walk?" Melissa asked, tucking a bookmark into her book.

"Yeah, we did. It's a really beautiful day outside."

"It seems like most days around here are beautiful in the summer." Melissa chuckled.

"That's definitely true. Such a welcome change from the city."

Charlotte looked around the living room, which looked much different than it had when she'd arrived. Her books were tucked neatly onto a low bookshelf that she had saved, Jean's diary sitting on the top of a stack of art books that Charlotte had placed for decorative purposes.

She bit her lip, then picked it up, going to sit next to her mother. Even though Charlotte had wanted to tell her mother about the journal, she hadn't imagined how she would do it. Melissa was always composed, but that was under normal pressures. Learning how much her sister had wanted to make things right after decades, and now not having the chance to was a different situation entirely.

But it was right to tell her, and soon. Now was a better time than any.

"What's this?" Melissa asked.

"I found Jean's diary," Charlotte said, holding the leather-bound journal in her lap. "And I've been reading it."

Melissa's brows furrowed, almost so subtly that Charlotte didn't notice. "You have?"

"Yeah." Charlotte swallowed "I know some of what happened between you and Jean."

Melissa went quiet and still, her eyes glued to the diary. She had spent so many years walled off, trying to appear as perfect as she could, that Charlotte found it hard to tell if she was surprised or scared or something else.

But now, Charlotte understood why. Her mother probably felt like letting go and being vulnerable about the real reasons why she had gotten divorced would open her up to judgment. After all, her sister and Charlotte's father were two people that were extremely close to her. Maybe Melissa figured that people would whisper behind her back, wondering why she hadn't connected the dots sooner.

Plus, two people she thought she could trust had, in her mind, betrayed her. It would have been hard to show any cracks in her armor, even in front of her daughters.

"Jean really loved you." Charlotte flipped to the back, where she had clipped the un-sent letters that Jean had addressed to her mother. "I found these letters that she wrote you but never sent. It didn't feel like my place to read these since they were for you."

Melissa took the letters, still quiet and hard to read. Giving her a tiny bit of space on the couch, Charlotte watched her tear the letters open. It only took a few moments after reading the first letter for her mom's carefully constructed facade to fall. Tears slid out of her eyes, slowly at first, then turning into full-blown crying.

Charlotte wasn't sure of what the letters said, but she could have guessed based on the multiple diary entries where Jean had written about her sister, wishing her apologies and explanations could make it through to her.

"Mom..." Charlotte hopped up to get some tissues, then offered them to her mom.

Melissa nodded in thanks and blew her nose with a honk that was very much unlike her. Charlotte rubbed her back. She had to be overwhelmed. She let her mother gather herself again without saying a word.

"I held a grudge for so long. For *decades*," Melissa said, her voice still thick with tears. "I gave up what could have been a good relationship with my sister because of it."

Charlotte didn't know what to say, so she just put her arm around Melissa's shoulder.

"Have I been too hard on you?" Melissa asked after another pause.

"No. Your encouragement pushed me to try harder and challenge myself. It's been hard, but worthwhile," Charlotte said. "But sometimes it feels like you want me to have a certain kind of life, like with a fancy job in a big city. It would be good if you could see that different people want different things out of life. I think staying in this town would be enough for me." Charlotte shrugged. "I don't need riches or fame or any big markers of success. I just need my friends and the beach and this town."

After a long pause that had Charlotte's heart climbing into her throat, Melissa nodded.

"I think you should stay too," she finally said. "You obviously love this town and the people in it way more than you loved Chicago. Being here seems like the right move."

Charlotte's face lit up. "Really?"

"Really. But maybe you could live a little bigger here too. You should try to buy The Book Nook and keep it open. I think with your experience, you could run it. Daisy clearly trusted you."

Charlotte blinked, too shocked to do anything else. But soon, the shock was replaced by excitement, then again by nerves.

"Are you serious, though?" Charlotte asked.

"Of course I am. I know you could do amazing things with it. From the looks of things, you were already doing a wonderful job."

Melissa squeezed Charlotte's hand as Charlotte took a moment to gather herself this time. It was a lot to think about—owning and running a bookstore was a huge thing to take on. Working with Daisy had shown her that there was so much work involved. It wasn't just making sure books were in stock and that the events ran. She had to anticipate her customers' needs, stock the *right* books, ensure the customer service was perfect, and a million other little things that she was going to need some help with down the line.

But it was doing well before Daisy's collapse, so clearly the town wanted a bookstore. Charlotte could keep it going well.

Feeling a spark of inspiration, Charlotte grabbed a notebook so she could bounce ideas off her mother and make plans. Since Charlotte had already done so much to modernize the store, she could keep going on that track. There was more than enough demand for more events, book launches, or even parties to add other streams of revenue with ease. An hour flew by.

"I think I can do it," Charlotte said, looking at the list of ideas she had put together. The page was filled. "I want to do it."

She looked up as she heard a vehicle coming down the driveway. It was Briggs.

CHAPTER TWENTY-THREE

Charlotte hopped to her feet when she saw his truck park. She had to tell him what she was going to do with the bookstore, hoping he would stay a little longer to help her see it through. Just as he burst out of his truck, she threw the front door open. They ran toward one another, meeting in the middle, their chests heaving.

"I need to tell you —"

"Wait, I need to get this out," Briggs said, cutting her off. He never did that, and Charlotte could tell that he was just as anxious as she was. She took his hands, almost instinctively. "Sorry. I'm just...this is a lot."

"Take your time." Charlotte squeezed his hands.

He took a few moments, steadying himself and

gathering his words. They were standing so close to each other that Charlotte could see the freckles that had popped up on his face from the sun and the smile lines around his eyes.

"You've brought so much light back into my life, Charlotte," he said quietly, but firmly. "Waking up every day feels so good again, like I want to tackle each day since you're in it."

"You've brought light into my life too." Charlotte smiled, feeling a little tension fall from her shoulders. "I thought I was doing okay before, but in retrospect, I can tell that I was just going through the motions instead of legitimately living."

"Yeah, it's just like that. I was numb for so long that I forgot that wasn't normal." Briggs chuckled softly. "I thought dragging myself out of bed and willing myself to smile along and nod was the best I could do."

Charlotte nodded. While her past didn't have as much tragedy as Briggs's did, she knew what it was like to look up one day, months having gone past without her really noticing or feeling anything different. Now she finished every day and could look back on it with a smile.

"I didn't think I'd ever feel love like this again, but I am," Briggs said after a pause.

"Briggs..."

Charlotte squeezed his hands, pulling him closer. Her throat was tight with emotion, as much as she wanted to tell him that she felt the same way. When she thought about it more, she realized that she had never felt like this for anyone—the easy way she felt around him, the comfortable silences, all the times he made her laugh and feel safe. She could be entirely herself and know that he would accept her. She was in love with him, and the realization was overwhelming in the best way.

She had an intense urge to kiss him, but she didn't want to cut him off.

"It almost feels like fate," he continued. "Right after I helped you get your car out of that sand on the side of the road, I felt like I'd found the right place. I figured it was just the beautiful scenery and small town charm, but maybe part of me was drawn here because of you."

Charlotte dabbed at her eyes with the back of her hand as tears swelled up in them. His words had summed up everything she was feeling and more, but she still couldn't speak without bursting fully into tears.

"I guess this is a long-winded way of saying that I love you." Briggs' cheeks flushed in a way that was so endearing that Charlotte's tears spilled over. "Oh, Charlotte..."

"No, no, they're happy tears." Charlotte sniffed and laughed as Briggs wiped away her tears with his thumb. "I love you too."

"That's a relief." Briggs laughed. "For a moment there I thought I scared you."

"No, you could never scare me with sweet words like that." She leaned into his touch.

"Good, because this might be a little scarier."

Briggs let go of her other hand, digging into his pocket for something. For a moment, Charlotte's heart started pounding all over again. Was he going to propose?

Instead, he pulled out a piece of paper and handed it to her, a nervous smile on his face. Looking at him with a furrowed brow, Charlotte took it.

"What's this?" she asked, clearing her throat.

"Just open it."

Charlotte unfolded the paper and quickly skimmed it. There was a lot of legal language, but she could tell what it all meant at a glance. It was a deed to the bookstore.

Charlotte pressed her hand to her chest, feeling a little woozy from shock. Of all the things she expected, this wasn't one of them. Even a marriage proposal felt more likely, even this soon. It took a few more moments to soak in, but she finally managed to look up at Briggs, struck speechless for what felt like the tenth time that day.

"This is what I went to do," Briggs said, his smile widening. "I bought it from Daisy."

* * *

Seeing the look on Charlotte's face made it all worth it. She went a little pale, then her cheeks flushed. For a moment there, Briggs thought she was going to faint and he gripped her elbows, just in case. But soon, her shock was replaced with elation. He smiled, taking her shoulders in his hands to steady her even more.

He had already been convinced that he loved her before, but now he knew it without a shadow of a doubt.

"I don't want to move on from here. I don't want to keep running." He tucked a stray piece of hair behind her ear. "I want to stay here and build something good with you."

"But how...but...it must have cost..." Charlotte blinked away a few tears, looking between him and the paper several times.

"I've had money from the settlement I got after my wife and son's death, just sitting there in an account, never touched."

"Briggs..." Charlotte's eyes stayed on his, almost in disbelief. "That's so much. I can't take this from you."

"I seriously hadn't touched it and I never thought that would change," Briggs said. "But now I can see that I was just waiting to use it for something that mattered. And this really matters."

Charlotte could only nod, more tears falling from her eyes faster than Briggs could sweep them away with his thumb. She was still struck speechless, but he could tell that his words were slowly sinking in as he'd wanted them to. He was surprised at how much he'd become attuned to her emotions already—she had reacted just as he expected.

Charlotte wasn't the kind of woman to expect gifts, so of course she tried to refuse him at first. But she also listened to him better than most people had, and she trusted him.

Everything he had said was true. He could tell how much Charlotte loved her job at the bookstore, and books in general. Hearing her happily talk about her days selling books and her fun with her book club made him happy, just by proxy. If there was a way he could keep that smile on her face and that purpose in her day, he was going to do it.

The amount of love he felt for her far exceeded his fears. Some were still there, yes—he hadn't been in one place for more than six months in ages—but he knew he could tell Charlotte about his fears. And they could share their hopes and dreams and everything they wanted.

"I'm not going anywhere, Charlotte," Briggs said. "Will you stay here with me?"

"Yes!" Charlotte threw her arms around him. "I want to stay more than anything else in the world. Thank you, Briggs. Thank you."

As they hugged, Briggs noticed Melissa standing on the porch, giving them an approving smile.

CHAPTER TWENTY-FOUR

Charlotte checked the time and started to panic a little. The night of the grand re-opening of the bookstore was finally here, and despite all of her careful planning and work over the past month, it felt like there was still so much to do.

The bookstore's name was the same in honor of Daisy, but Charlotte had made sure to put her own stamp on things. She'd changed the layout so it was easier for customers to walk in and see the newest releases.

She'd kept a few of Daisy's plants, but added a few little knickknacks and figurines that she had saved from Jean's house. The last few outdated chairs in the reading corner had been given a fresh update with a reupholster that Addison had helped her with, and she and Briggs had painted the bookshelves to add more life to the store.

Briggs had also done a few repairs and made some new book displays that were perfect for the front window. Now Charlotte could change it much more easily and show off more books.

The final touch, a last minute gift, were the big flower boxes that Briggs had somehow made, right under her nose. With some help from Sadie, who had more of a green thumb than Charlotte, she had planted some brightly colored flowers.

It had been hard working in all of the little updates since the store hadn't been closed the whole time, but they had made it work. Some nights they'd been there past midnight, but Charlotte got up at six each day to get to the store early, regardless. It was exhausting, but she had never felt so alive in an odd way. She never had to push herself to get things done, but she tried to maintain as much balance as she could.

It helped that Briggs had been amazingly supportive in helping her relax whenever she could.

Some evenings, in the rare times that she was able to have a night in to rest, he cooked dinner for her. He only had a few recipes up his sleeve, but all of them were delicious. After dinner, they sat in some chairs out back and watched the sunset, just enjoying each other's company and the view.

They started as many mornings as they could with walks on the beach with Bruno, who Charlotte also couldn't imagine living without. He had started sleeping at the foot of her bed, his soft snoring lulling her to sleep. When winter came, he was going to be an excellent cuddle buddy.

Once the shop was officially re-opened, she wanted to see how he'd do if he came to the bookstore with her, at least once or twice a week. The more she brought him around people, the more she realized how good he was with pretty much everyone. Having him around, brightening her and her customers' days, was something she was looking forward to now that the shop was officially hers.

This was their big "hard launch" where they had invited the community in to celebrate the store's new life—she wanted everything to be as great as possible. As much pride as she'd had in her past jobs and even working at the store, now that she was the owner, her feelings had been taken to a whole new level. Her belly fluttered, filling with nerves.

"Let's see, let's see," Charlotte murmured to herself, looking over the list of things she had to do.

The food and drinks were in her office, waiting to be put out on the tables in the book club room, which had gotten a fresh coat of paint. They had put signs guiding people to the room just in case it got too crowded. Since the store wasn't that big, they had moved a lot of things around to give everyone a bit more breathing room.

She had also gotten some well-known authors to come and do signings, and they had let her know they were in the area. Charlotte's former coworkers had graciously helped to connect her to a few of them, some who were so famous that Charlotte was a little nervous to meet them. Since the space was a little chaotic with Charlotte, Briggs, and her friends bustling around, the authors were waiting in a nearby coffee house until the doors opened.

She smiled to herself. Some of the other women from book club were massive fans of an author who had committed last minute, so they had no idea the author was coming. They were going to freak out when they heard.

Then, something that Charlotte had forgotten about clicked in her head—the gift bags that she had put together for the authors, plus their signing tables upstairs. She rushed around, double checking that the author stations had enough Sharpies and their gift bags were in place. Luckily she hadn't forgotten everything, though now she was worried that something else was slipping her mind.

"You okay?" Briggs asked, poking his head into the room. His blue eyes were gentle.

"Just a little worried. I made a comprehensive list and I'm just afraid that I've missed something somehow." She walked toward Briggs, who took her hand and led her downstairs.

"You've been doing a great job. Trust me, you haven't left any stones unturned." Briggs squeezed her hand and released it. "Everyone's going to love it."

Charlotte cracked a smile. "Thanks, Briggs."

Charlotte watched him help Addison prepare the front desk for more purchases, then looked over her to-do list again. Next up was food.

"Hey, would you mind helping me bring out the food?" Charlotte asked Sadie as she passed by, a box of flyers for the store's upcoming events in her arms.

"Yep, just let me put these down!"

Charlotte went to the back and started grabbing the wine, then Sadie came to get the coolers of food. Despite the strength she had gained from picking up boxes and boxes of hardcovers, Charlotte had drastically underestimated how much the wine weighed.

"Woah, hold on," Briggs said, spotting Charlotte struggling with the box. "You're going to hurt yourself or send a bunch of bookshelves falling to the ground."

"Thank you." Charlotte off-loaded the box of wine bottles into Briggs' arms, which he hardly struggled with at all. "Wow, you make it look easy."

"It's pretty heavy, not to mention gigantic. I'm surprised it didn't crush you." Briggs grinned over his shoulder at her and brought the wine to the snack table.

"Hey!" Charlotte laughed, playfully smacking his arm. "I lift boxes of books all the time. I was just a little too ambitious."

"Well, that ambition has been really helpful." Briggs put the box down and started pulling out a few bottles of each drink. "Just not for moving boxes of wine."

"True."

Charlotte was able to grab the mini bottles of water for people who didn't want alcohol or sparkling water, and she, Briggs, and Sadie went to work arranging everything so people didn't have to wait to get a drink. Soon, the table was perfect—besides the drinks, there were mini-pastries and cookies from her favorite coffee shop, and Elise had arrived with warm appetizers from her father's restaurant that all of them had to sample first.

"So good." Charlotte sighed, savoring the bite-sized puff pastries, topped with a delicious spread that Charlotte loved, but couldn't place—it was a little savory, with a gentle fruity sweetness that balanced it out. "What is this, Elise?"

"It's prosciutto, cheese and berry jam. Dad's secret recipe." Elise popped one into her mouth. "Whenever we describe it on the menu, people are a little confused, but it works well."

"Like a mini charcuterie bite?" Briggs asked, reaching for another one but stopping himself.

"Yeah, just like that!" Elise straightened the platter and took a step back. "Looks great!"

"It really does." Charlotte looked around. Everything seemed to be in order, and the doors were going to open soon.

Briggs pulled Charlotte into his arms, giving her a hug before pressing a soft kiss to her lips. They hadn't been together long, but Charlotte had the feeling that his kisses were going to make her heart feel fluttery for a long, long time.

"I'm so proud of you. And all of this," he said, still holding her close. "It looks great. And very 'you', without losing Daisy."

"It wouldn't have been possible without you." Charlotte squeezed his forearms.

"No." He shook his head, his eyes warm and smiling. "You would have found a way to make it work. I'm sure of that. I'm just glad I was able to help you out in some way."

Charlotte's phone buzzed in the pocket of her skirt, interrupting the kiss she was going to place on Briggs's cheek. It was the alarm to notify the authors to come to the store. Once they arrived, the doors would open.

"It's almost time!" Charlotte said. She quickly contacted each of the authors and showed them inside. Once everyone was in place, she took a deep breath and opened the door to the small crowd gathered out front. "Welcome, everyone!"

She stepped back, letting people in. Nina and Melissa were right at the front, looking around at the shop with wide eyes.

"Charlotte, it looks so amazing!" Nina said, throwing her arms around her sister.

"Yes, it does," Melissa agreed, looking around. "You've done so much since the last time I was here.

It looks truly incredible. Look at how bright it is! And this layout looks so nice, though I'm guessing you'll have to move a few things back after the event. Either way, it's so inviting."

"Thank you." Charlotte's heart warmed, especially at her mother's compliments and the pride in her voice. Her mother hadn't always loved her choices, but there was no denying that she was supportive of Charlotte in that moment. "I'm really proud of it."

"We're totally in the way, aren't we?" Nina laughed and stepped to the side so more people could trickle in.

"Go explore—there are authors mingling around before their signings later and there's wine." Charlotte gently pushed Nina toward the back and Melissa followed.

Charlotte greeted everyone as they came in, saying hello to people she recognized from book club, which was now back from its brief hiatus, and people she had met through Sadie, Elise, and Addison. The small store was quickly becoming packed, with people browsing the aisles and sipping their drinks.

Briggs was right by her side, chatting with people and guiding them to the part of the bookstore they were interested in. On occasion, he looked at Charlotte and smiled.

"Hey, Charlotte," Ethan said, coming into the store and looking around. "Wow, everything looks great. Congrats."

"Thank you!" Charlotte beamed. "Feel free to look around or have a little wine and refreshments. The author book signings will be starting in a little while upstairs."

As she spoke, she noticed Ethan shift his gaze from her to Briggs, who was chatting with someone about a thriller that the store had just gotten in stock. Charlotte was standing so close to Briggs that she could feel the sleeve of his shirt against her arm. It was a comfortable distance, though she knew that it must have looked very familiar to someone else.

A smile curved Ethan's lips when he turned his attention back to her. Understanding gleamed in his eyes, as if he should've known she and Briggs were meant for each other ever since he mistook them for a couple in his office.

"Refreshments sound great," he said with a nod. "And where can I find nonfiction? Maybe true crime?"

"To your left, where Sadie is." Charlotte

gestured to where Sadie was talking with someone else from book club.

"Thanks. Congrats again." Ethan gave a small wave and kept moving.

The influx of guests had slowed down a little, so Charlotte did a lap around the store, saying hello to people she had somehow missed and making sure that the food and drinks were still fresh. Soon she ended up back at the front, right as Daisy and Elise's father Arthur appeared.

Seeing Daisy's face light up as she saw the bookstore, before she noticed Charlotte, made Charlotte's night. It was almost as if she couldn't believe it was the same store. Both Daisy and Arthur were looking more energetic and spry, as if they'd finally got the rest they both deserved. It looked like taking things slower was working out for them both.

"Charlotte!" Daisy said, waving.

Charlotte pulled Daisy into a long hug. "I'm so glad you made it!"

"I'm glad I did too." Daisy looked around again. "It looks so amazing in here! Thank you for keeping the shop alive. I had been so sad to close it, but this is perfect."

"So you like what I've done? I changed things a little bit."

"Of course!" Daisy gently squeezed Charlotte's shoulder. "It's your place now. It *should* change. You're bringing the store into a whole new generation. The only way it can continue on is if it changes, you know?"

Charlotte smiled, feeling surprisingly choked up. "Thank you, Daisy."

"Good luck, Charlotte. If you'll excuse me, I see there are those little charcuterie bites that I love back there." Daisy laughed and disappeared into the crowd.

"Daisy was pleased?" Briggs asked, handing Charlotte a small bottle of water that she had wanted but hadn't had a chance to grab yet.

"Yeah, she was! She looks so much better, doesn't she?" Charlotte looked over her shoulder, trying to find Daisy again, but she had been swallowed by the crowd.

"She does." Briggs slid his arm around her waist and gave her a little squeeze. "I bet seeing her store in such good hands has helped her feel more at ease too."

He kissed Charlotte's forehead and she leaned against him, looking at the gathered crowd. She had never expected this place to become her permanent home, but it had. Feeling Briggs at her side and seeing everyone laughing, smiling, and talking about books drove the sense of belonging home for her. Nothing could make her happier.

She couldn't wait to see what the future would bring.

ALSO BY FIONA BAKER

The Marigold Island Series

The Beachside Inn

Beachside Beginnings

Beachside Promises

Beachside Secrets

Beachside Memories

Beachside Weddings

Beachside Holidays

Beachside Treasures

The Sea Breeze Cove Series

The House by the Shore

A Season of Second Chances

A Secret in the Tides

The Promise of Forever

A Haven in the Cove

For a full list of my books and series, visit my website at www.fionabakerauthor.com!

ABOUT THE AUTHOR

Fiona writes sweet, feel-good contemporary women's fiction and family sagas with a bit of romance.

She hopes her characters will start to feel like old friends as you follow them on their journeys of love, family, friendship, and new beginnings. Her heartwarming storylines and charming small-town beach settings are a particular favorite of readers.

When she's not writing, she loves eating good meals with friends, trying out new recipes, and finding the perfect glass of wine to pair them with. She lives on the East Coast with her husband and their two trouble-making dogs.

Follow her on her website, Facebook, or Bookbub.

Sign up to receive her newsletter, where you'll get free books, exclusive bonus content, and info on her new releases and sales!